WANTED: ONE WEDDING DRESS

They had the dress...all they needed were husbands

On her very special day there is nothing more important to a bride than having an exquisite wedding dress. The wonderful dress in Sharon Kendrick's trilogy was designed and made by Holly's mother (ONE BRIDEGROOM REQUIRED!) and bought in anticipation by the mother of Amber (ONE WEDDING REQUIRED!) and Ursula (ONE HUSBAND REQUIRED!). For the lucky husbands-to-be, it was a dress that made their fiancées look drop-dead gorgeous!

Dear Reader

Planning a wedding is like writing your first book—you should stick with what you know! We were flat broke when we got married, and the only way to guarantee a show-stopping dress was to have it made for me (refusing to accept that my curvy shape looked *nothing* like the supermodel on the front of the pattern!). So I bought slippery satin and filmy organza and the dress was made, and...

And I looked like a whale!

Two weeks before the ceremony, I had to rush out and buy a replacement dress. Luckily, I found one—but I ended up with two wedding dresses and a lot of extra expense!

With weddings it's best to play safe...

At least until after the service is over!

Sharon Kendrick

ONE HUSBAND REQUIRED!

BY

SHARON KENDRICK

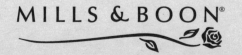

MILLS & BOON®

To the Fabulous Fozards—
Baz (Benito), Gill (Wigs), George, Franny and Tot

First published in Great Britain 1999
Harlequin Mills & Boon Limited,
Eton House, 18-24 Paradise Road, Richmond, Surrey TW9 1SR

© Sharon Kendrick 1999

ISBN 0 263 81684 2

Set in Times Roman 10½ on 12 pt.
01-9906-50325 C1

Printed and bound in Spain
by Litografía Rosés, S.A., Barcelona

PROLOGUE

THE wedding dress gleamed pearl-gold in the morning light. Finest silk-satin and sheer organza. A drift of tulle, like a summer cloud. Ursula ran her fingers lightly over the plastic cover which protected it, and sighed.

It was sleek, stark and stunning—the perfect gown to make a beautiful bride. Ursula's mother had bought it for her daughters for just that reason, but Ursula knew in her heart that she would never wear the dress.

For a start it was much too small.

And the man she loved was married to someone else...

CHAPTER ONE

July

'URSULA?'

'Yes, Ross?'

'Um…are you doing anything on Saturday?'

Ursula O'Neil was a practical woman who usually ran on automatic pilot until at least midday. But this one question was enough to make her hand hover over the telephone. She looked up at her boss in amazement.

It was the 'um' as much as the question itself that made Ursula sit up and take notice.

Six years of working for a man meant you got to know him pretty well. He could be distracted when he was working, irritable on a deadline, and soft as butter with his daughter—but Ross Sheridan hesitating? Never!

Words were his business, his stock-in-trade. What Ross couldn't do with a few words wasn't worth knowing… He could make you weep, or giggle, or rush out to buy a certain brand of dog food—even if you didn't own a dog! These days he was Chairman of the agency, true, but at heart he was still a simple copywriter.

And a man who never hesitated.

Ursula forgot all about the telephone call she had been about to make. 'Would you mind repeating what you just said, Ross?'

Ross studied the pencil which was positioned between his long fingers like a spear. Then he looked up and smiled, and Ursula was caught in the crossfire of eyes so dark they were almost black. Inky, brilliant and unforgettable.

But the eyes were obscured by a frown. 'I *said*, are you doing anything on Saturday?'

Well, he wasn't asking her for a date, that was for sure. But Ursula allowed herself the brief and guilty fantasy that he was before she said, 'Well, no, I'm not, as it happens. Why?'

'We're having a party.'

'You're having a party?' she repeated carefully.

'That's right.'

'Where?'

'Where do people usually hold parties? At home, of course.'

'Oh. I see.' But she didn't. Ross and his wife had held parties before and never bothered sending her an invitation. So why the sudden change in behaviour?

'And I wondered whether you'd like to come along?'

Ursula continued to gaze at Ross, as if seeking clues for the invitation in a face which was much too interesting to be described as merely handsome. But it came pretty close...

'Me?' she squeaked, realising as she said it that she sounded like some latter-day Cinderella!

'Yes, you,' he agreed, frowning even more. 'For pity's sake, Ursula—I've never seen you so lost for words before! What do you think's going to happen? I'm not planning to cosh you over the head and sell you off to the highest bidder!'

Interesting fantasy, decided Ursula.

He leaned back in his chair. 'Have I shocked you so much by asking you?'

'Not shocked,' she corrected primly. 'I think it would take a little more than that to shock me, Ross! Bemused might be a better description. I mean, in all the years I've worked with you—'

'Please don't remind me how many!'

'I won't.' Years which had just blurred and flown. The reality of just how many should have disturbed Ursula far more than it seemed to disturb Ross—but then she never let herself stop to think about it. Because then she might start thinking she was in a rut and that it was time for a change.

And she didn't want to change. For who in their right mind would ever change the perfect job and the perfect boss?

'Ever since I first entered the mad, mixed-up world of advertising...' she smiled '...and you plucked me from the obscurity of the general office to become your personal assistant—'

'And?' he cut in impatiently, as he was in the habit of doing if he thought something was irrelevant. 'What's that got to do with me asking you to a party?'

'Well, you've never invited me to anything at your house before.'

'That's because you once told me quite emphatically that you didn't like to mix business with pleasure!'

Ursula thought about this for a moment. 'That's true,' she admitted. Well, true that she had *said* it, not that she had *meant* it, of course. Not deep down. It had been a survival technique to protect herself from the buckets of charm her boss possessed. She could have quite happily spent every evening in Ross's company if the truth were known. Every lunchtime. Every breakfast. Every waking hour if she was being embarrassingly and brutally honest, and only one thing stopped her.

He was married.

And even if he wasn't married—*even if he wasn't*—there

was no way he would look twice at *her*. Men like Ross Sheridan were never attracted to women with unfashionably curved bodies of softly cushioned hips, and breasts which looked like overripe melons. They liked their women slim. No. Skinny. With plenty of bones showing, like sleek race-horses. Classy women.

Like Jane. Ross's wife.

Jane, who was tall and creative and possessed the kind of qualities which readers of teenage magazines were always aspiring to. Jane who could throw on a tatty old dress bought from the thrift shop and look like a million dollars in it.

Swallowing down whatever stupid emotion it was which had caused her throat to constrict, Ursula stared at her boss. 'So what's it in aid of—this party?'

For the first time in all the time she had known him Ursula saw Ross's face grow slightly uncomfortable, as if he couldn't quite make up his mind how to answer. So. First hesitation. Now tension. And all in the space of a single conversation. How very odd.

'We promised Katy that she could have a birthday party,' he drawled. 'And Jane thought it might be a good idea to swell the numbers. Invite a few adults. And I immediately thought of you.'

'Ah!' Ursula smiled with pleasure. 'Now I see!'

Katy was Ross's daughter and Ursula loved her to bits. Sometimes he brought her into the office with him during the school holidays, when Jane was extra busy. Katy liked to trot round after Ursula like a little dog, and Ursula genuinely enjoyed her company.

She had taught Katy how to use the computer, and to play gin rummy, and in return Katy kept her up to date on the current fashions and music scene! It only seemed five minutes since the *last* birthday, when—come to think of it—Ursula had accompanied Katy and Ross on a trip to London Zoo. She screwed her nose up as she tried to remember. Now where had Jane been *that* day?

'I can't believe her birthday has come around again!' she told him. 'She'll be eleven, won't she?'

He shook his dark head. 'Ten.' He twirled the pencil like a drum majorette's baton, in the way he always did when something was on his mind. 'She just looks older.'

'Acts older too,' observed Ursula thoughtfully as she thought about Katy's remarkable self-possession. 'She's a very grown-up young lady, and she knows more about fractions and base numbers than I ever will!'

'Well, that doesn't say very much,' mused Ross, a glint of mischief lightening his dark eyes, 'since you are the most mathematically challenged person I know!'

'If that means I hate anything to do with figures, then you're right!' Ursula observed the twirling movement he was continuing to make with his fingers. 'Is something wrong, Ross?'

His fingers stilled and his eyes narrowed warily. 'Wrong?' he repeated suspiciously. 'What makes you ask that?'

If she admitted to studying his body language, and detecting an edginess simply by looking at his hands—then wouldn't that make her look a bit sad? 'You just seem a little preoccupied this morning,' she told him truthfully. 'You have done all week, to be honest.' Indeed, all *month* if she was being brutally honest.

'You know me too well, Ursula,' he said quietly, only it sounded more like an accusation than a compliment.

'Well?' She ignored the warning look in his eyes. 'What's the matter?'

'My deadlines are mounting—'

'Then delegate!' she told him sternly. 'You're the Chairman of the agency, for heaven's sake!'

'But the client wants *me*.'

That was the trouble—the client always *did* want him. 'Well, the client may not be able to have you!' she glowered. 'They may have to use Oliver instead, or one of the many creative whizkids you pay huge salaries to!'

'We'll see.' He gave a dismissive shrug, then turned on his lazy smile. 'So will you come, Ursula? Katy would love you to be there.'

Ursula only pretended to think about it. She *had* always refused to attend social events when they were connected with work, but this was the first time he had ever invited her to his *house*. She told herself that it was simply a genuine desire to help Katy celebrate her birthday which had her itching to attend. And it was. But deep down she was dying for a glimpse into his home life. Would he be as messy as he was in the office? Would Jane be clucking round the kitchen like a mother hen? 'Thanks very much. I'd love to come.'

'Good.'

'What time on Saturday?'

'About six o'clock? We promised Katy that she could have an early-evening party.'

There it was again, the 'we' word, reminding Ursula— if she had *needed* any reminding—that Ross was already spoken for.

'So no jelly and ice cream?' she questioned lightly.

'Oh, I wouldn't say *that*! If you're very good, I'll see if I can organise chocolate cake!' He grinned back and began to draw funny little shapes onto the large sheet of paper in front of him, which told Ursula that he was about to go into creative mode.

Unusually—and lucratively—Ross Sheridan managed to

combine the twin accomplishments of being artistic and yet having a strong head for business. In the competitive world of advertising he was already a bit of a legend—and he was still only thirty-two! As a copywriter, he was second to none—his the dizzy success story which others aspired to. As people said—any campaign with Ross Sheridan's name on it was Midas-kissed!

His rise had seemed effortless—but Ursula knew how hard he had worked to get to where he was today. He had started out at Wickens, one of London's biggest agencies, where he had quickly established himself as one to watch. Early on he had produced two brilliantly successful ads which had gone on to win national awards. That was where he had met Ursula, who had been temping because the money had been better and she had needed as much as she'd been able to get her hands on.

In Ursula, Ross had recognised talents which complemented his own. She was punctual, efficient and sensible. She didn't spend hours on the phone to her boyfriend or come back from lunch all giggly with wine.

When Ross had left Wickens he had taken Ursula with him—to the buzzy 'hotshop' agency where all the brightest talents had converged, and where Ross had met Oliver Blackman. And when Oliver and Ross had formed Sheridan-Blackman—their own breakaway agency—Ursula had been their first full-time member of staff.

She'd been with Ross so long that sometimes she felt like part of the wallpaper—while at others it seemed that her life with him had sped by in a flash. And the one great constant was his charisma. That never dimmed, just kept drawing you to him, like a moth to the flame.

Like all creative personalities, he had his flaws. He could be irritable and exacting, short-tempered and impatient. But he compensated with his enthusiasm, his brilliance and the occasional smile which could make grown women swoon.

She looked at him now, trying to analyse his appeal.

Every day was dress-down day at Sheridan-Blackman, and today Ross was wearing trousers which made his legs look spectacularly long. He wore these with an open-neck shirt which couldn't disguise those lumberjack shoulders or the lean body which every woman in the building dreamed of.

He topped six feet in his bare feet—which everyone knew because he often kicked his shoes off after arriving at the office! His hair was lighter than black but darker than brown—wavy, thick and usually in need of a trim.

Ursula sighed. It wasn't easy working for a man who looked as if he should be starring in a jeans commercial!

Forcing herself to concentrate on something else, Ursula rose to her feet. 'Do you want some coffee?' she asked him.

'Coffee sounds good.'

She was almost at the door when he said, 'Ursula?'

She turned round, noticing blue-black shadows beneath his eyes, and thinking that he looked as if he needed a good night's sleep. 'Yes, Ross?'

'Any chance of a couple of aspirin to go with that coffee?'

When he turned those big dark eyes on her like an abandoned puppy, there was every chance that she would grind the chalk to make the tablets herself!

'Hangover?' she quizzed sweetly. 'Or some ongoing complaint I should know about?'

He scowled. 'I just asked you for a couple of pills—I didn't expect to have you carry out a full medical on me!'

Unwanted, X-rated thoughts went sizzling across her mind, but Ursula didn't miss a beat. 'Yes, boss,' she said crisply. 'You just carry on sitting there quietly relaxing while I run around and fetch for you.'

'Thanks,' he replied absently, scribbling on a notepad and not seeming to notice the sarcasm in her voice.

In the office's adjoining kitchen, Ursula ground some coffee beans, then plugged the kettle in. She looked out of the window at the London skyscape as she waited for it to boil, reflecting on how lucky she was to work slap-bang in the centre of London, and in such a stunning suite of offices. For a girl with just a clutch of typing certificates to her name she hadn't done too badly!

Like the rest of the building, the kitchen had been designed with the kind of flair you would expect from an advertising agency. Glossy and slick. As Ross had informed her on her first day at Wickens, 'Image is everything in this business.' Ursula remembered that he had said it in a very cynical, jaded kind of way, and she recalled wondering whether he was happy or not.

She remembered the day she had discovered that he was married, with a young daughter, and the great stabbing feeling of disappointment she had felt. Which had been utterly ridiculous when she had thought about it afterwards. Surely she hadn't been expecting that a dreamy hot-shot like Ross would be interested in a plump Irish orphan like *her*?

But having her hopes dashed—however futile they had been—had meant that she had gone on to develop a strong working relationship with her boss, one that wasn't based on false expectations of having him clasp her in his arms one day! That wasn't to say that she didn't still sometimes have the occasional little fantasy about him—but she wasn't alone in *that*. So did every other woman in the building!

'What's happened to the coffee?' came a low growl from

the office. 'Are you boarding a plane for Colombia to harvest the beans yourself?'

Ursula smiled as she popped two aspirin out of their foil container, poured him a glass of water and carried them through to him.

He looked pale, she thought critically, handing him the drink and the tablets.

'Thanks.'

'Are you ill, Ross?'

He shook his head. 'Just sleep-depleted.'

'Well, don't frown,' she told him sweetly. 'It'll give you lines,' and went back out to the delectable smell wafting from the kitchen before he had time to come up with a smart reply.

Pinned on one of the walls of the kitchen was a framed still of one of Ross's most successful campaigns, featuring a glossy young blonde with bee-stung lips, sipping from a glass of iced cocoa. The blonde had been sitting on a beach, clad in the skimpiest of bikinis, and Ross's copyline had read, 'Not Just For Bedtime...'.

The campaign had exploded the myth that cocoa was only drunk by fuddy-duddies. It had also started a hot and angry debate in the women's pages in newspapers about whether it wasn't time to stop using sexist images to sell products. Ross had refused to comment.

Sales had shot through the ceiling, and Ross had become the hottest property in town—and in more than just a commercial sense. With his creative genius, a body that was lean and hard—and eyes which could sometimes resemble hell's fire—Ross Sheridan was the man whom everybody wanted to be seen out with.

Except that he was seen out with nobody because he had a wife and daughter at home!

And Ursula admired him for that. Over the years, the

man had had enough temptation put in his path to have tempted the holiest of saints. She had seen models and actresses coming on to him like nobody's business. But Ross hadn't just resisted—he had shown absolutely no interest.

Which only added to his appeal. The irresistible man who was beyond temptation. Moody, spiky, brilliant and erratic.

She carried the tray of coffee through, added a plate of his favourite biscuits. She had poured them both a cup and settled back down at her desk when his deep voice punctured the silence.

'Ursula?'

'Yes, Ross?'

'Um, how old are you exactly?'

Ursula blinked. Again, the uncharacteristic use of the word 'um'. 'But you *know* how old I am!'

His mouth assumed a stubborn little-boy curve. 'Not *exactly*, I don't,' he hedged obstinately.

'How exact do you want? Down to the nearest minute? Are you plotting my horoscope for me?'

'Very funny.'

'Don't you know that it's rude to ask a lady her age?'

'But I don't know any ladies,' he mocked. 'Only women.'

The velvet sensuality which underpinned his words had the undesirable effect of making Ursula's cheeks grow scarlet.

'Ursula,' he teased, 'you're blushing.'

'Well, you caused it!' she snapped.

'Only because you were being so coy about your age.'

'That was not coyness!' she returned. 'It was a perfectly natural wish to keep something of myself back!'

'Oh, I wouldn't worry about that. You keep plenty of yourself back,' he remarked obscurely, and took a sip of his coffee before catching her in the inky crossfire of his eyes. 'So are you going to tell me?'

Ursula found herself wondering briefly whether there was *ever* an age that a woman was happy to admit to! 'I'm twenty-seven—twenty-eight soon.' She stared across the room at him. 'Why do you want to know?'

He batted her back an innocent look. 'Does there need to be a reason?'

Ursula shrugged, and the upward movement caused her long dark hair to catch the light in a blue-black gleam. She wore her hair loose and flowing around her shoulders—not a terribly practical style for work, but at least it diminished the width of her unfashionably round face. Or so she thought. 'Of course there needs to be a reason!' she told him. 'I've worked with you for the past six years and you've never bothered asking me before!'

'Maybe I'm planning to surprise you—'

'You mean you're going to turn up on time tomorrow morning?'

He laughed, but it was a slightly uneasy laugh. 'You're right,' he sighed. 'I *have* been late a lot recently.'

Ursula quickly straightened the papers on her desk into a neat line. She wasn't going to ask why. Didn't need to. Married men who kept turning up late in the morning usually had a very legitimate reason for doing so—presumably because they had been distracted by the womanly wiles of their wives.

And that was an area of Ross's life which Ursula determinedly kept her nose out of. She was glad that Ross was happily married—she just didn't want it rammed down her throat every five minutes.

'So why the sudden interest in my age?' she quizzed. 'Have you decided that I'm due a pay rise as a reward for long service? Or maybe just for being long-suffering?'

Ignoring her question, Ross picked up a pencil and with three swift, hard strokes on a sheet of scrap paper managed to produce an uncanny likeness of a philandering Cabinet Minister who had been in the news all week. 'It's disturbing,' he said, after a minute, 'to think of you getting on for thirty.'

'It is *very* disturbing,' Ursula agreed equably, 'when you put it like that. Because I'm not! Now who's the mathematically challenged one? I happen to be more than two years *off* thirty! I'm not exactly queuing up for my pension just yet! And, besides,' she added defensively, because taking a resolute attitude helped diminish the fear of a lonely old age, 'thirty isn't very old, not these days.'

'No. You're right. It isn't.' His voice was thoughtful as he fixed luminous dark eyes on her. 'And is there a man on the scene?'

Ursula blinked with surprise. What on earth was the matter with Ross today? First inviting her to Katy's party. And now this. He had *never* asked her about her love life before. 'Y-you mean…a *boyfriend*?' she asked breathlessly.

Ross gave an odd kind of smile. 'Do you only go out with boys, then, Ursula?'

If only he knew!

But no one knew, not even her sister, though Ursula suspected that Amber must have guessed her embarrassing secret. That she had reached the grand old age of twenty-seven and had only ever had one serious boyfriend. And even he hadn't been *that* serious; not if you judged the relationship in the way everyone else did—in terms of sex. Because—shame of all shames—in a liberal world where experience was everything, Ursula O'Neil remained an out-of-touch virgin.

'No, there isn't a boyfriend,' she told him, hoping she didn't sound too defensive. 'I'm quite busy enough with my line-dancing and my French Appreciation lessons. And I read a lot. I don't need a man to justify my existence, you know!' She frowned at him suspiciously. 'And why have you suddenly started taking an interest in my personal life?'

'No reason,' said Ross innocently. He absently took a bite from his biscuit and then looked at it in surprise before finishing it, like someone who hadn't realised how hungry they were before they started eating. He popped the rest of it in his mouth and crunched it.

'Miss breakfast this morning, by any chance?' queried Ursula.

'How did you guess?'

'The way you practically bit your fingers off? That gave me just a tiny clue!'

He smiled as he licked a stray crumb off his finger with the tip of his tongue. 'You know, you're bright, funny and extremely tolerant, Ursula.' There was a pause as he looked across his desk at her. 'Do you ever think about changing your job?'

Ursula might have felt insecure about her looks and lack of attraction to the opposite sex, but she was supremely confident about her work, and it didn't occur to her that Ross might be hinting at her to leave. She assumed an expression of mock shock. 'You really want me to answer that? On a Monday morning, when you've got a headache? What's up, Ross—worried that I'll walk out and leave you in the lurch?'

'I'm serious, Ursula.'

'Well, so am I.' She blinked at him, dark, feathery lashes shading her unusually deep blue eyes. Her best feature, or so her mother always used to say. 'I *presume* that wasn't a prelude to ''letting me go'', or whatever horrible euphemism it is they use these days when someone wants to sack you! Was it?'

'*Sack* you?' He gave a gritty smile. 'I can't imagine the place without you, if you must know.'

Which sounded like a compliment, but left her with a rather disturbing thought. 'Do *you* think I'm stuck in a rut, then, Ross?'

'The question rather implies that other people do,' he observed. 'Anyone in particular?'

'My sister,' Ursula admitted.

Ross knitted his dark brows together. 'Amber? The model?'

'She doesn't really model very much these days—not since she got herself involved with Finn Fitzgerald—'

'But she doesn't approve of you working here?'

Ursula bit her lip, wishing that they'd never started this wretched conversation. Life was so much easier if you just drifted along without asking too many questions along the way. 'She thinks six years in one place is a long time.'

'And she's right,' he said slowly.

Ursula looked up in alarm. Maybe she had misjudged things. Him. Maybe subconsciously he *did* want her out.

Ross saw the wide-eyed look of fear on her face and shook his head. 'Now what's going on in that pretty little head of yours?'

'Don't you patronise me!' she snapped. '*Or* tell a lie!'

'And how am I telling a lie?'

'I am *not* pretty!'

'Well, that's purely subjective, and I happen to think you are—exceedingly.' He saw her blush, and smiled. 'In fact, if I go so far as to be *objective*—then I'd describe those enormous eyes as sapphires set in a complexion as dewy and as fresh as creamy-pink roses left out in the rain—'

'Now you're letting your copywriting skills run away

with you!' she interrupted drily. 'Just what are you trying to say to me, Ross? That our working partnership has grown stale? That there's some hungry new female champing at the bit to replace me, and you *do* want me to go?'

Ross sighed. 'No, I don't want you to go. Right now, all I want is to resist the temptation to make any comments about female logic. Or the lack of it,' he added in a dark undertone. 'But I *am* interested in hearing your sister's objections to you working for me. Particularly since I've met her on very few occasions. She hardly *knows* me!' he finished indignantly.

'Oh,' she said, with an evasive shrug of her shoulders. 'You know.'

'No, Ursula, I don't.' He looked at her.

'She…she…'

'She…?' he put in helpfully.

She didn't dare tell him her sister's *real* reason for urging her to leave Sheridan-Blackman. That Amber thought Ursula was being unrealistic. Wasting her life by pining for a man who could never be hers. Except that I'm *not* pining! Ursula thought defiantly. *Or* being unrealistic.

Just because she happened to like Ross as a man, and enjoyed working with him—it didn't necessarily mean she wanted to start ripping his clothes off! 'She thinks that a change of scene would do me good.'

'It's worth thinking about,' Ross said unexpectedly.

'It *is*? Then that *does* mean—'

'It doesn't mean anything,' he put in impatiently. 'Other than that it might be an idea to consider any other offers which may come your way.'

Other offers? Ursula stared at him in confusion. 'But they're not likely to, are they? Not if I'm not actively seeking employment. I'm a personal assistant, not an account executive, and I'm hardly a prime target for head-hunters!'

'I guess not,' he answered tersely. 'Do you have a lot of work to do, Ursula?'

'Not particularly.' She tried to answer lightly, but it wasn't easy now that he had sown seeds of doubt in her mind. Somehow she had gone from complacency to insecurity in the space of about half an hour. 'Otherwise I wouldn't be sitting swopping idle chit-chat with you.'

'Then maybe you could pop down to the market and buy me some oranges?'

She didn't miss a beat—but then she was used to bizarre requests by now. 'How many?'

'A dozen.'

'And these oranges—are they for eating, or looking at?'

'For looking at. I need inspiration! There's a new juice campaign coming up—and Oliver's pitching for the account. So we need to compose the perfect catchphrase which will have people ransacking their supermarkets for Jerry's Juice. So. Any brilliant ideas?'

Ursula knitted her brows together in concentration. What did *she* like best about orange juice? 'Everyone always emphasises how sweet it is…'

'Yeah. And?'

'Well, why not do the opposite—emphasise how *sharp* it is?'

'Any ideas?'

Ursula shrugged. 'Oh, the possibilities are endless—sharpens the appetite, that kind of thing. You know! *You're* the copywriter, Ross!'

'Mmm, I am,' murmured Ross slowly. 'But maybe you should be, too. You're in the wrong job, you know, Ursula.'

'No, I'm in the right job!' Ursula unlocked the petty-cash tin and took a ten-pound note out. 'Just because I happen to have a fertile imagination and an active mind doesn't mean I want to be a copywriter!'

He laughed. 'So you'll come to Katy's party on Saturday?'

'Oh, I wouldn't miss it for the world,' she promised airily.

CHAPTER TWO

THERE was a click as the connection was made. 'Hello?'

Ursula paused before saying, 'Is that you, Amber?'

'Of course it's me! Surely you know the sound of my voice by now! I *am* your sister!'

'You just sounded… I don't know…*odd*.'

Amber gave a heavy sigh which reverberated down the line. 'Just fed up. Finn's overworking. Again. How are things with you?'

'Er, fine.' Ursula hesitated. 'Ross has invited me to a party on Saturday.'

'Gosh. What does his wife say about *that*?'

Ursula silently counted to ten. She loved her sister very much, but sometimes, honestly… 'I have no idea,' she replied frostily. 'But I should imagine that he checked with her before he asked me. I do wish you wouldn't make assumptions, Amber. I'm hardly worthy competition, and anyway—I like Jane.'

'Yeah, sure.'

It was time, Ursula decided firmly, to put an end to Amber's totally false speculations about what kind of party Ross had invited her to. 'I do like her,' she reaffirmed, though more out of duty than conviction. 'What little I know of her. And anyway—it's Katy's birthday party.'

'*Oh.*'

'Why do you say "oh" in that tone of voice?'

'Oh, nothing. I suppose I imagined that he was whisking you off to some glamorous advertising-related function.'

'Well, he's not. And I never go to those, anyway.'

'So you've been invited to a child's tea party?'

'It's an early evening supper, actually.'

'Wow!'

'Don't be mean, Amber.'

'I'm not. I'm being objective. And protective.'

'Protective?'

'Of course. And it's slightly worrying that this… party…is your social affair of the month!'

'It isn't!'

'Well, what else have you done this month?'

Ursula even found *herself* cringing as she answered her sister's question. 'I went out for a meal with my French Appreciation class last week—'

'And were there any men there?'

'Lots!' said Ursula brightly, as she recalled the portly doorman from the nearby Granchester Hotel who sat next to her in class. He was planning to visit Marseilles for a holiday to trace some of his forebears and had grown hot and sweaty around the collar before asking Ursula if she wanted to accompany him on the trip! She had politely declined.

Then there was that rather nice young sculptor whose pint she always paid for if the class went to the pub afterwards, because he never had any money. True, he was only twenty—but terribly friendly. And very interesting.

'*Eligible* men?' put in Amber sharply.

'That's so subjective I can't possibly answer it!' responded Ursula smoothly.

'Well, if everything is so marvellous, then why are you ringing me, Ursula?'

'Because I don't know what to wear!' wailed Ursula.

There was a short silence.

'Oh, I'm not suggesting borrowing something of yours!' said Ursula hastily, sensing her sister's embarrassment. 'I wouldn't like to try and squeeze myself into one of your size eight Lycra miniskirts!'

'I'm a size ten now,' said Amber, the gloom in her voice suggesting a disaster of national proportions.

'Oh, that's *terrible*, sweetie!' teased Ursula, though she had to bite back her first comment, which was that she would be in seventh heaven if she were anywhere *near* that size! She had gained extra weight as a teenager, and never really lost it. 'But it doesn't help me to decide what to wear!'

She *could* have asked Amber how she imagined it must feel when your main criterion for buying any outfit was whether or not it made your bottom look fat and wobbly. But of course she couldn't do that. If Ursula's bottom was bigger than she would have liked, then it was nobody's fault but her own. If you ate too much, you got fat. Cause and effect. Simple. And, while she might occasionally justify her plumpness by calling to mind the grim reality of her growing-up years, nothing altered that simple fact.

'Wear jeans,' advised Amber succinctly. 'They're always useful around children.'

'*Jeans!* If I wore jeans, they'd be digging out their safari clothes—I look like a hippo in jeans!'

'Well, I'm not going through a whole list of suggestions just so that you can shoot them down in flames! What do you *want* to wear?'

Ursula's voice was unusually hesitant, and shy. 'Do you think the cream trousers and top you helped me choose would be okay? I haven't worn them yet.'

'Perfect!' said Amber immediately. 'The colour emphasises how dark your hair is, and brings out the roses in your cheeks. Oh, and clip your hair back at the sides with those mother-of-pearl slides I bought you for your twenty-first.'

'Okay.'

'Oh, and Ursula?'

'Uh-huh?'

'Be good!'

Amber's words echoed around Ursula's ears on Saturday evening, as she stood opposite Ross's house, trying to summon up enough courage to go up to the front door and knock. Be good, indeed! She didn't think she'd have a problem sticking to *that* advice! She doubted whether there would be any men there whom Amber would consider 'eligible', and even if there were they wouldn't spend a moment looking at *her*.

She swallowed nervously as she gazed up at the house. How she wished she'd had a drink before she had set out!

She hadn't even bothered asking Ross how many others were going, or who they were. She just prayed frantically that all the women weren't in the same kind of league as Jane, his wife.

She stared down at her toes poking through the strappy sandals which were the most summery shoes she had—an absolute necessity on a night like this. It was baking hot, even though the sun was getting low in the sky.

Ross lived in Hampstead, which was miles on the underground from Ursula's little flat in Clapham Common. It had been far too hot on the train, but not much better once she'd got off and begun to walk up the hill.

The air had a strange, almost suspended sense of stillness about it, with no breeze existing to lift it away. It had made her feel hot and bothered. Still did.

Ursula surreptitiously wiped her brow with the back of her hand, and the little hairs on the back of her neck prickled up, her senses on full alert, as if suddenly aware of someone watching her. She narrowed her eyes as she allowed herself a closer look at the imposing, late-Victorian house.

Someone was!

She glanced up and saw a figure blackly silhouetted against an arched window on the first floor and she could tell, even from this distance, that it was Ross. She studied him dispassionately, cushioned by the safety net of distance, thinking that the pose he struck highlighted the complexity which lay at the heart of the man. He looked both relaxed and yet alert.

Watching.

Waiting…

Well, there was no way she could possibly dawdle any longer, not without looking a complete idiot. Ursula clutched her handbag even tighter and, tucking Katy's birthday present under her arm, she crossed the road, went up the steps to the front door and banged loudly on the knocker.

It was opened by Katy herself, looking more grown up than her ten years in short blue denim skirt and a sparkly blue tee shirt, which looked expensive. She was a tall girl for her age, and the platform shoes she wore made her even taller.

Katy had her father's deep brown eyes and even deeper brown hair—but hers curled into wild corkscrews whereas Ross's just waved gently against the nape of his neck. Her wiry height she owed entirely to her mother, along with a nose which was a cute, freckled snub and rosebud-pretty lips.

'Happy birthday, Katy!' beamed Ursula, and held the present out towards her. 'I *love* your tee shirt!'

But Katy seemed more interested in a hug, hurling herself into Ursula's arms with a fervour which was as surprising as it was touching.

'Ursula!' she squeaked. 'You're the first here! I'm so glad you came! I *made* Daddy invite you!'

Ursula willed her face not to react, but there was nothing she could do to stop her heart from plummeting like a dropped stone. So it had been Katy's idea to invite her, had it? Not her father's at all... She just hoped that she wasn't going to stand out from the other guests like a sore thumb.

'I'm so glad I came, too—and I'm flattered to be invited,' she told Katy truthfully. 'I don't get to go to many birthday parties these days.'

'Why not?'

Ursula shrugged. 'Because grown-ups only tend to have parties when they're twenty-one, or forty—'

'How boring!'

'Very boring,' agreed Ursula gravely. 'Now open your present and tell me whether you like it,' she added gently. 'You can always change it if you don't.'

Katy needed no second bidding, immediately dropping to her knees and ripping the shiny paper off the carefully wrapped parcel with all the energy of a highly excited child.

Inside was a box of water-colour paints, a small packet of oil-pastel crayons, and a thick block of sketching paper. Katy sat back on her heels and stared at it.

'Do you like it?' asked Ursula nervously. 'I thought you were very good at drawing, just like your daddy—'

'Oh, I *love* it!' said Katy earnestly, looking up at Ursula with shining eyes. 'I really, really *love* it!'

Ursula smiled widely. 'That Christmas card you sent me last year was so good that I've kept it—that's what gave me the idea for the present. I keep meaning to have it framed.'

'Seriously?'

'Seriously.' Ursula nodded solemnly. 'You have a real gift for drawing, you know, Katy.'

'And does Daddy have a gift, too?'

'Oh, definitely. Your daddy's the best!'

'Why, thank you, Ursula,' came an amused voice, and they both looked up to see Ross at the top of the staircase watching them, making Ursula wonder just how long he had been standing there. 'How heartening to hear such praise—and this from the woman who usually nags me about my untidiness!'

'Only because if I didn't I wouldn't be able to reach my desk for the mountains of paper in the way!' she responded crisply, but her heart was beating faster than usual.

It was odd seeing him in the unfamiliar surroundings of his home. Their relationship had evolved in the everyday environment of the office, and even when they had a client lunch in an upmarket restaurant it was strictly business. Transplanted here, with not a work-related product in sight, she felt like a fish out of water!

Feeling slightly flustered, but hoping it didn't show too much, Ursula scrambled to her feet with as much grace as she could muster. 'This is an amazing place you've got here, Ross!'

Why was he studying her like that—as if they were meeting for the first time? She suddenly felt as uncertain as a teenager as she wondered what he saw. His frumpy assistant? Or a reasonably well-presented young woman?

The silk trousers and top were the pale colour of buttermilk, and Amber had been right—the creamy shade *did* emphasise the blackness of her hair. The design of the outfit was deceptively simple, fluidly skimming the curvy shape of her body—and the delicate fabric felt unbelievably soft where it clung to her bare skin. And although the outfit was practical, it was also intensely feminine—the kind of clothes she wouldn't have *dreamed* of wearing to the office.

Was that why his eyes were out on stalks like that?

'Hello, Ursula,' he said softly. 'Nice outfit.'

'Th-thanks.' She smiled uncertainly.

'It's unbelievable,' he murmured. 'You look completely different, dressed like that!'

'Whereas you look exactly the same!' she shot back, wondering what on earth they were supposed to do *now*. And why was Katy just standing there, serenely watching the two of them? Why wasn't she interrupting, the way children were *supposed* to do?

At work, Ursula could bury her feelings in a flurry of activity, but here there was nothing to buffer her from the impact of Ross as a man, rather than an employer. Was he oblivious to the fact that he was a highly desirable man?

'Where's Jane?' asked Ursula quickly.

'Mummy's going to be late,' said Katy, in a sulky voice. *'Again!'*

'Jane's been tied up at work, unfortunately,' said Ross, his voice as smooth as a pebble.

'Not literally, I hope!' joked Ursula, but her feeble joke didn't even raise a smile and left her wondering why she had bothered making it, until she realised that her fingertips were now trembling with nerves.

'She's doing the costumes for the new Connection tour,' Katy informed her, sliding a shy hand into Ursula's.

Ursula's eyes were like saucers. 'The Connection? Wow! Their last album was brilliant! I'm impressed.'

'Well, don't be! They're all self-obsessed substance abusers!'

'Katy!' exclaimed Ross, looking shocked.

'Well, *you* were the one who said it, Daddy!'

'Not in front of you, I didn't,' he told her grimly.

The ringing of the front doorbell sounded like salvation, and Katy beamed with delight when she discovered five of her school friends standing on the doorstep.

'We all came in Mum's station wagon!' exclaimed one. 'Polly's bought you the soundtrack from *Musketeers!*'

'Thanks for spoiling the surprise!' grimaced Polly.

'Oh, it doesn't matter—I'm far too old for surprises,' said Katy airily. 'Come on, shall we go next door and play it?'

'Great!'

'And Sally's bought you the *Musketeers!* video!'

'Great!'

Squealing with excitement, the girls ran off, and Ursula was left alone in the hall with Ross in a space which was probably almost as large as the office they shared, but which now seemed claustrophobically confined.

'They seem nice girls,' she commented, hoping that she didn't look as awkward as she felt. 'Katy's friends.'

'Yes.'

She saw the brief but unmistakable glance he sent at his watch. 'Can I do anything to help, Ross?'

He seemed to switch on a smile with an effort. 'Sure. You can come into the sitting room and have a drink with me.'

She shook her head. 'I meant, do you want me to cut the crusts off the sandwiches—or ice funny faces on cup-cakes?'

'I know what you meant, and, no, I don't. But thanks, anyway.' He smiled more as though he meant it this time. 'Children's parties have changed since our day. I'm afraid that your prediction of no jelly and ice cream is completely accurate! I suggested it to Katy and she did a convincing impression of someone about to throw up! And then in-formed me that they'd like to ring out for pizza!' He sighed dramatically. 'Kids' parties ain't what they were in our day!'

'I wouldn't know,' said Ursula, without thinking. 'I never had a birthday party when I was growing up.'

He looked quite shocked. 'What—*never*?'

'Never!' Ursula's mouth twitched. 'You think that's such a terrible thing?'

'It's certainly rather unusual. Why not?'

'Oh, you don't want to know.'

'Don't tell me what I don't want, or what I do want! You can't clam up on me here, Ursula—we aren't at work now.'

'No.' Because if they had been they wouldn't be talking this way. Softly. Intimately. With Ross's possessions all around only adding to this unwelcome familiarity…

'So why no parties?'

Ursula gave him a wry look. 'You are a very persistent man!'

'I need to be.' He studied her carefully. 'Because you never seem to want to talk about your childhood.'

'Well, come to that—neither do you!' she retorted. 'I thought we were there to work—not have in-depth therapy sessions!'

'Tough, was it?' he queried softly.

'Parts of it,' she hedged, because she didn't want him thinking she felt sorry for herself. 'My mother was a widow—and her whole life was spent juggling jobs in order to provide for me and Amber. She was worn out most of the time, and every single penny counted, so a birthday party would have been right out of the question. But Mum sometimes used to make a cake and stick a few candles in it, and the three of us would finish the lot!' There was a long pause. 'The last time she made a cake, Amber was about Katy's age.'

'And then?'

She stared at him. 'You want to hear the whole thing?'

'Don't you want to tell me?'

Ursula hesitated. 'When we were in our teens my mother got sick,' she said baldly. 'She was ill for a long time. She died last year.'

'And you cared for her, I guess?'

She looked at him in surprise, then nodded. 'Yep. Nursed her at home until just before the end.'

'I see,' he said slowly. 'That explains a lot.'

'Oh?' Her fingers moved up to check the mother-of-pearl slide which clipped back a great handful of black hair. 'Like what?'

'Your kindness. Your maturity. Other things, too, but you're right—' he gave her a gentle smile '—this isn't a therapy session. Let's go and have that drink now. You look like you could use it.'

'That sounds good.' But she hadn't found his questions invasive at all. It had been almost a relief to tell him. Sometimes you locked away the bad, sad bits of your life so that they festered, like a sore.

She followed him from the hall into one of the reception rooms, where leaded windows gave the room an old-fashioned look which was enhanced by the blaze of colour from the garden beyond. The style of the room remained as simple as the large hallway they had just left—with polished floorboards strewn with rugs, and carefully chosen, non-matching pieces of furniture which gave the room a very modern appearance.

There was an already opened bottle of champagne on ice, and Ross gestured towards it. 'Like the best boy scout, I came prepared. How about some of this?'

Ursula wasn't really the kind of person who drank chilled champagne before the sun had even gone down, but she certainly wasn't going to ask him for a glass of beer!

'I'd love some,' she said.

He poured them both a flute and handed her one, and Ursula took it over to the open French doors, to have a better look at the garden. It was large enough to require both passion and dedication to have it looking as good as that, she decided.

'So who does the gardening?' she asked him. 'You or Jane?'

'Oh, Jane hates gardening,' he told her, with an odd kind of laugh. 'She likes cut flowers bought from expensive florists and wrapped in pretty paper! She has an aversion to mud and bugs!'

'And what about you?' she quizzed curiously. 'Do you have an aversion to mud and bugs?'

He smiled. 'On the contrary—I like the feel of the soil on my hands. There's something very satisfying about planting something in the ground and watching it take root and grow. No, my excuse for employing someone else to do the garden is that any free time I have, I prefer to spend with my daughter.'

He had moved slightly closer to her, and Ursula could detect the faintest trace of aftershave—a combination of musk and lemon which somehow seemed more heady out here in the open air than it ever did in the office. He must have been in the shower shortly before she arrived, since his hair was still very slightly damp.

Ursula shivered, in spite of the sun still beating fiercely down on their heads. She began to long for someone else to arrive, almost as much as she hoped that no one would.

She took a hurried mouthful of champagne. 'So is anyone else coming to the party?'

'You mean more children?'

'I meant more adults.'

'Just Jane,' he told her. 'And whoever she decides to

invite at the last moment—which leaves the field wide open.'

She ignored the caustic tone in his voice. 'No grandparents?'

'No. Like you, my parents are both dead. And Jane's are divorced—she doesn't see her father, and her mother lives in Australia.'

'No godparents?' She saw the tightening of his features. 'I'm sorry—I didn't mean to pry.'

He shook his head. 'That's okay. It's natural enough to ask. We've never actually had Katy christened. Jane has a horror of organised religion.' He took a sip of champagne. 'You obviously disapprove.'

'My opinion doesn't matter,' she told him frankly, then smiled and raised her glass. 'But I'm honoured—to be the only other adult invited!'

There was a pause. 'And what if I told you that I had lured you here under false pretences?'

Ursula felt her heart bashing against her ribcage as wild fantasies sprang into rampant life. 'In what way?' she croaked.

'Just that Jane sometimes gets carried away with work, forgets about the time, that sort of thing—'

Ursula suddenly understood. 'And you needed someone you could rely on, to pick bits of pepperoni up off the floor?' Someone, moreover, who would not read too much into the invitation—because Ursula was certain that there must have been tens of women who would have been delighted to step into Jane's shoes for an evening and mastermind a children's party…

'Someone with the organisational skills to co-ordinate a game of musical statues, actually.'

Ursula hid a smile. 'I think you'll find that ten-year-old girls will find musical statues too "babyish".'

'You reckon?'

'Yes, I do.'

Ross had gone quite pale. 'Then what do you suggest we do with them for the next three hours? I didn't bother hiring an entertainer!'

Ursula smiled. 'Don't panic! Right now they're listening to a CD, and at that age they have the capacity to listen to it over and over again—for hours on end! Then they'll probably want to watch the video while they eat their pizza. They'll want us adults as far away as possible—they're quite easy to please, really.'

'You aren't a secret mother by any chance?' he teased. 'With a brood of children hidden away at home?'

'No.' It was an image which stubbornly refused to be credible, but not because she couldn't imagine herself as a mother. Simply that she had terrible difficulty conjuring up the idea of anyone as the father... 'But I brought up my sister when our mother became too ill.'

'But now that Amber has flown the nest...you don't have anyone to take care of?' he said softly.

'I don't need anyone to take care of!'

'Oh, yes, you do! You were born to care, Ursula,' he told her gently, and appeared about to qualify this extraordinary statement, when they heard a key being turned in a lock and then the sound of voices, and muffled laughter.

Silence.

Whispers.

Then more laughing.

'That must be Jane,' said Ross abruptly, just as his wife came into the room, closely followed by four men wearing rather theatrical clothes.

Musicians, thought Ursula immediately.

'Hi, honey!' smiled Jane breezily, and blew Ross a kiss. 'Who's this?' She narrowed her eyes in Ursula's direction.

'Oh! It's you! The indispensable assistant!' She gave her a brief nod. 'Hello, Ursula!'

Ursula pressed her lips together in a smile. 'Hello, Jane. Nice to see you.'

Jane was very easy on the eye, the kind of woman about whom other women always said, 'I don't know what people *see* in her!' But Ursula knew exactly what people saw in her. Men especially.

It wasn't just that she was tall and skinny, or had hair so thick and curly it resembled a lion's mane. Or a mouth so wide her smile could dazzle you. Not that she smiled very often, mind you—certainly not when Ursula had met her. No, her looks were more than a total of her parts—she had that indefinable quality called style, which could not be bought.

Today she was wearing green velvet hot-pants and a tiny matching bolero, which only just covered her small breasts. Her midriff was bare and smooth—lightly tanned to the colour of cappuccino—and Ursula wondered whether Ross *minded* his wife walking around the place dressed like that—like a teenager who had worn the outfit for a dare.

Ursula looked again at the four men, whose long hair and deathly pallor proclaimed them as rock stars, and even Ursula—who wasn't really a star-spotter—sucked in a breath of disbelief when she spotted that one of them was Julian Stringer, lead singer of The Connection, his wild green eyes slitted as he drank deeply from a bottle of beer.

Ursula watched him with fascination, thinking that he had that total disregard for the conventional which only the *really* famous ever displayed.

He sensed Ursula watching him and his eyes widened slightly, and in that moment she understood exactly why women all over the world threw their underwear on stage whenever he was in concert.

He wasn't really tall enough to be described as conventionally good-looking. He had the hips of an adolescent boy and the shoulders of a man, and his hair spilled untidily around his face and shoulders. But he had a kind of mad, wild beauty, with his too-white skin and bright green eyes, and you could sense the passion which ran beneath that rather twitchy exterior. He wrote savage love songs with haunting tunes. No wonder people fell in love with him, thought Ursula.

He turned to Jane. 'Want us to play something for your kid, baby?' he drawled. 'We've got all the gear outside in the van.'

'Wow! Would you really?' Jane looked at Ross with excitement. 'What do you reckon?'

Ursula knew Ross well enough to know when he was angry, and right now she could see that he was absolutely *furious*.

'I don't think that now is the right time for an impromptu gig from The Connection,' he answered repressively.

'Oh?' Julian Stringer scowled like a petulant child. Last summer they had topped the Billboard charts in the States, and he was *not* used to having his offer to play for free turned down! 'Like to tell me when *is* the right time, then, man?'

Jane laid her hand on Ross's and Ursula saw him tense up. 'Ross,' she said softly. 'It's a great honour to have Julian and the boys play for us. Think what a treat it would be for Katy! It would be a birthday she'd never forget!'

'You mean, it would be a birthday *you'd* never forget,' argued Ross, then gave a weary sigh as his wife opened her mouth to object. 'Okay, go ahead. Ask Katy.'

Katy and her friends were ecstatic, and didn't make any attempt to be cool.

'Julian!' they squealed in excitement when they saw him. 'Can you play ''Space in my Heart''?'

Adulation was obviously what Julian liked most. He removed his lips from the vacuum of the empty bottle and grinned for the first time, and Ursula found herself thinking that if *she* had all his money and teeth that looked like *that*, then she would invest in a decent orthodontist at the first opportunity!

'Sure can. I can play you anything you want. Wanna get the gear in?' he mumbled to the rest of the band.

But the rest of the band were in the process of opening bottles of champagne. They were tired from touring and lack of sleep, and had no intention of doing anything other than getting drunk on this sweltering evening.

'Give us a break, Julian! It's too hot, man! Why don't you just sing something with the acoustic guitar?' suggested the dark one with the heavily tattooed shoulders and a small diamond studded into the centre of his tongue.

It was, Ursula reflected as Julian tuned up, just unfortunate that he had drunk so much. His voice was flat and out of tune and his phrasing was incoherent. And halfway through his chart-storming hit he actually forgot the words!

Clustered at his feet sat a circle of small girls, looking confused. 'It doesn't sound *anything* like the record!' whispered one.

Ursula couldn't decide whom she felt most sorry for. Katy. Or Ross. Or Julian Stringer.

'Maybe we should ring out for pizza now?' suggested Ross impatiently, as the number came uneasily to an end.

Jane glared at him. 'Don't be so rude, Ross. I don't think that Julian's finished playing yet!'

Ross's face remained calm. He looked at his daughter and her friends. 'So what's it to be, girls? Pizza? Or more music?'

They looked at each other like conspirators. *'Pizza!'* they shrieked in unison.

Jane bent her head to speak. She spoke very quietly, but Ursula heard it all the same as Jane hissed into her husband's ear, 'You bastard! I'll never forgive you for this, Ross!'

And Katy heard it, too. Her mouth trembled.

'Why don't you show us all the rest of your birthday presents while we're waiting for the pizza, Katy?' Ursula suggested brightly.

Suddenly, she just wanted to go home.

CHAPTER THREE

IT TOOK a few days before Ursula felt back to her normal, cheerful self after Katy's birthday party. Seeds of discontentment had been sown onto exceptionally fertile ground. She found herself asking *why* Jane Sheridan didn't count her blessings and rejoice in having a gorgeous daughter and an equally gorgeous husband instead of behaving like a spoilt child.

Left to Jane, the party would have fizzled out like a damp firework.

Julian's disastrous solo had produced instant sulking, not just from Jane, but from Julian, too. Ursula had overheard him complaining about Ross—whom he'd blamed for the 'bad vibes' which apparently were responsible for him forgetting the words to a song *he* had written. This had led to all kinds of silent, angry looks being projected across the room by the main protagonists.

'This is *your* doing!' Jane snapped at Ross. 'You've just ruined Julian's creative flow! You can't *bear* to think that somebody else might be the centre of attention, can you?'

'You mean other than Katy?' he queried evenly. 'Whose birthday it happens to be?'

Ursula stole a glance at Ross. She had never seen him quite so angry—even though he was doing a pretty good job of hiding it. But Ursula was an expert on Ross's face—she'd studied it in so many different guises! And she could see that it was taking every bit of self-restraint he possessed to appear pleasant.

Ursula began to grow impatient with the atmosphere. It

was supposed to be a child's party, for goodness' sake—not a wake! The Connection had now started drinking red wine, and she dreaded to think how drunk they would get if they didn't have something to eat pretty *soon*. She could have wept with joy when she heard the approaching sound of a motorbike as it screeched to a halt outside.

'That'll be the pizza!' she said brightly, and saw Katy perk up. 'Lead me to it—I'm absolutely *starving*!'

'Ye-es.' Jane raised her eyebrows at Julian. 'I expect you must be—'

Julian snorted with laughter. 'Yeah! Right! It takes a lot of fuel to stoke a big engine—am I right, baby?'

Ross narrowed his eyes. 'I think you'd better—'

'Ross!' Ursula's voice rang across the room, and they all turned to look at her. 'Don't,' she beseeched him. 'It doesn't matter what anyone says about me. Honestly.'

But Ross shook his head, his voice full of quiet determination. 'Oh, yes, it does,' he contradicted stubbornly. 'I won't stand here and have you insulted, Ursula.'

'But I'm sure that Julian didn't mean to be *unkind* to me,' said Ursula, sending the rock star an innocent look of understanding which soon had him blushing with discomfort. 'Did you?'

'Er…no,' mumbled Julian, fumbling around in his jacket until he found a cigarette and jammed it into the corner of his mouth. ''Course I didn't.'

'I mean, I *do* have a very healthy appetite,' agreed Ursula. She sent a rueful gaze down at her curvy figure in the creamy trousers and matching top. 'As you can see for yourselves!'

'Healthy?' queried Jane archly. 'Having more than ten per cent body fat is hardly what I'd call *healthy*!'

'But I suppose that substituting meals with black coffee and cigarettes is?' Ross challenged.

Jane's whole demeanour altered. Perhaps she sensed that out-and-out aggression wasn't getting her anywhere. Whatever it was, her whole persona seemed to transform itself before their eyes, as she became sex-kitten and super-wife rolled into one. 'But I've stopped smoking, Ross,' she told her husband in a husky voice. 'You *know* I have.'

'Really? Well, in that case you won't mind that I chucked away the carton I found hidden in the understairs cupboard?' he queried innocently.

Jane's mouth became a thin line that for a brief moment looked almost ugly. 'Oh, for God's sake—do you *have* to be such a control freak?' she snapped. 'Going around checking up on me!'

He didn't react. 'Tempers seem to be getting a little frayed,' he observed calmly. 'So why don't we all eat something?'

'Didn't you say we could eat outside if it was sunny?' questioned Katy, jumping to her feet.

Ross smiled at his daughter. 'Of course we can! Why don't you girls take some rugs out onto the lawn?'

Katy and her friends seemed pleased to have a distraction from the simmering discontent provided by the adults. Ursula helped Ross carry the cardboard boxes of warm pizza out onto the lawn, while Jane and The Connection organised trays of drinks.

'Don't forget the cola, Mummy!' called Katy plaintively. 'We're not old enough for wine!'

Ursula thought that they made an ill-assorted gathering, all lying on plaid rugs beneath a sweet chestnut tree and swatting at the occasional wasp which dared to dive-bomb the pizza. The children, Ross and most of The Connection ate heartily, and Ursula limited herself to just two delicious pieces, then sat licking her fingers. But Julian continued to swig from a beer bottle, staring at Jane intently, while Jane ate nothing at all.

Once they had staved off their hunger, the girls began to grow restless.

'What can we do, Ursula?' asked Katy.

Ursula had been expecting this. 'Why don't you each bring me back seven different leaves?' she said. 'And I'll award a prize to the child who finds the most interesting one! But please don't take any from a plant which looks already bare!'

'Bags I look down by the Wendy house!' yelled Katy. She kicked off her impractical platform shoes and ran bare-foot over the grass, looking her true age at last, and not just a scaled-down version of a grown woman.

Ursula hastily excused herself and went off to explore the walled garden, glad to escape the fractured atmosphere herself. She thought how parched the flowers looked against the warm, red bricks. The heat was bouncing off the walls, sizzling behind the sweet peas which were massed in a fragrant blaze of mauve and pink.

She stopped by a sundial and slowly traced her finger round the metal circle of the clock. She was peering closer to see how accurate it was when a dark shape fell over the clock face, and she looked up to find Ross standing there studying her, his expression shadowed and heavy.

They looked at one another in silence.

'Well, go on, then—' his voice sounded raw and grazed '—say it.'

'Say what?'

'What you're really thinking—or are you afraid it will hurt me too much?'

'I don't imagine that the truth would hurt you,' she said slowly. 'I was thinking about how hot it was, if you must know, and before that...'

He was very still. 'Yes?'

'Before that I was wondering how you could bear to have Jane bring that band to your daughter's birthday party.' She shrugged. 'Though I guess she could say the same thing about me.'

'The difference is that you're a positive asset at a party, while Julian and the others are a bunch of self-indulgent idiots! But that's probably how she'll seek to justify it,' he agreed.

Ursula looked at him in bewilderment. 'You make it sound like a *war*, Ross!'

'No.' His look was sceptical, his laugh bitter. 'Just a marriage.'

He sounded so *disillusioned*. 'But if it's like that, then…'

'Then, what? We have a child, you know, Ursula.'

'Yes, I know.' And to children, parents meant stability. Hadn't she once read somewhere that a child was often the glue which held a marriage together? Was that the case here?

He was still looking at her. 'Ursula—' he began. 'About Jane and Julian—'

'I know what you're going to say, Ross, and it doesn't matter.'

'How can you possibly know what I'm going to say?'

She pushed a damp strand of hair back off her hot cheek. 'That you're sorry if I was offended by any of the many references they made about my weight?'

'Well, that too,' he offered drily. 'It was damned rude!'

'Don't worry, I'm used to it.'

'Oh?'

'Sure,' she shrugged. 'People often tease me. Sometimes the things they say are flattering—like telling me that Rubens would have adored to have painted me. And telling me that skinny women don't have pure, clear skin like mine.'

'Well, while we're on the subject, you *do* have an extraordinarily fine complexion.'

Ursula smiled. 'You *see*?'

'But what gives people the right to think they can say things like that to you?'

'It's because I'm not big enough to be labelled as obese, so they think I don't care—'

'But you do care?'

She gave him a steady look. 'What do you think?'

'I think that you should wear that colour more often,' he told her unexpectedly. 'It makes your hair look *sensational*.'

'That's exactly what my sister told me!' She screwed up her eyes suspiciously. 'Unless you're just saying that to make me feel better.'

'I'm not in the habit of telling lies.'

'No. I know you're not.' She looked at him with frank eyes. 'Isn't it unbearably chaotic, Ross, living like this?'

'What you're seeing today is not a normal family day, Ursula. Things have been rather different since Julian Stringer exploded onto the scene,' he said carefully. 'And for once in my life I can see the wisdom in waiting.'

She sensed that he wanted to close the subject, and so she asked him nothing further.

That night, after Ross dropped her off at home in his shiny emerald sports car, Ursula was unable to settle. She wandered around her little flat, restlessly plumping up the already neat cushions, and rearranging the fresh flowers she had bought from the market only that morning.

She was meticulous about her home, but then it was more than just a home to her. It was her nest and her haven, and she had worked very hard to get it. When her mother had become so ill, she had had to grow up fast, persuading the social services that she was fit to take on their mother's role and care for Amber herself.

She had learnt to type at school, and had taken well-paid temporary office jobs until she had found her niche at Wickens—and found the boss of a lifetime in Ross. Working with Ross had given her a security she'd never known before—both emotional *and* financial.

She had salted away every penny she could save, and when the opportunity had risen to buy their mother's council flat very cheaply Ursula hadn't hesitated. At first, it had been more than a struggle, but fortunately Ursula had discovered that she possessed a natural flair for budgeting!

And house prices in the area had shot up. The estate had been cleaned up and revitalised, and last year not long after her mother had died, Ursula had sold the flat for an obscene profit. It had left her with just enough to buy her current home in leafy Clapham Common. The small flat had been occupied by squatters and had been almost derelict—hence the knock-down price—and Ursula had poured much of her energy into creating the neat and gleaming little home it was today.

She put the kettle on to make some tea, and thought back to the evening, reflecting that Ross certainly did not appear to have the idyllic family home life she had always imagined. But wasn't life a bit like that? You always thought that everyone else was having a more exciting and fulfilling time than you.

She sipped her tea and remembered some of the things Jane had said to her. Ouch! The comments about her weight had been brutal, but she hadn't spoken anything but the truth, and Ursula wondered if she was on her way to becoming a figure of derision. A thoughtful but frumpy woman who was fast-tracking towards her thirties with an empty future looming ahead.

Her sister had settled down with Finn Fitzgerald and seemed ecstatically happy, and, consequently, Ursula didn't see very much of Amber these days. Maybe it was time for her to try to find a man of her own—and the French Appreciation class sure wasn't going to throw up a selection of suitable would-be partners! Not if past experience was anything to go by.

Ursula cleaned the make-up off her face and spent a long time showering, then carefully hung the cream silk trousers and top up in the wardrobe so the creases would fall out. She sat up in bed sipping tea and trying to concentrate on the glossy magazine she'd bought at the tube station that morning, but for once the enticingly entitled articles failed to grab her attention.

She *was* in a rut, no doubt about it. Maybe she should do what a lot of other single twenty-seven-year-olds did and join a dating agency...

Ross was in a filthy temper; that much was clear when he stormed into the office just after ten.

Ursula looked up from the pile of post she had been steadily working her way through.

He took one look at the stack of envelopes and scowled.

'Fan mail?' he growled.

Ever since he had been profiled in a TV programme about the rewards of working in advertising he had been besieged with requests for interviews and tips from wannabe tycoons.

'Sort of,' she prevaricated. 'Maybe you should just write a book entitled *Get Rich Quick Without Working!*—I'm sure it would be an instant international bestseller!'

'I'll bear that in mind,' he said evenly. 'In between ferrying my daughter to and from school, trying to find a new cleaner, attempting to write a witty speech for the Advertising Awards ceremony—as well as putting in my fair share of hours here!'

'That sounds like good old-fashioned moaning to me,' she observed in surprise, because Ross usually managed to shoulder a heavy workload without batting his outrageously long, dark eyelashes.

'*Moan!*' he exclaimed. 'Now why on earth should I want to moan?' He yawned and tipped his head back. 'I'm bushed, Ursula!'

Ursula picked up an imaginary violin and began to play it. 'Oh, poor, poor Ross!' she sang softly. 'My overworked boss! While the rest of the country takes pleasure in shirking—the industrious Sheridan never stops working!'

'Very funny.' A smile twitched the corners of his mouth. 'Actually, that wasn't bad, considering you made it up on the spot. Maybe I should delegate the copywriting to you— since you have such an abundance of hidden talents!' But his words were barely coherent as he stifled another yawn. '*And* I need a haircut. What's in the diary for tomorrow?'

'Meetings, meetings and more meetings,' she told him apologetically. 'And in the afternoon it's—'

'Let me guess—more meetings?'

'Afraid so.'

Ursula gathered up a clutch of papers and carried them over to him, thinking that, yes, he *did* look tired. Not like Ross at all. 'So why are you ferrying Katy to school?' she asked. 'I thought Jane usually did that.'

'She does. But not much lately, unless under extreme duress. Lately, she's been too busy making costumes for the forthcoming Connection tour. And, of course, nothing is ever good enough for Julian Stringer.'

'Oh,' said Ursula indistinctly, feeling vaguely uneasy at

something in the tone of his voice, without knowing why. 'Is it a *long* tour?'

His laugh sounded hollow, almost regretful. 'There are dates all over the world—and Julian's spending a fortune on staging. I think the special effects are meant to divert attention from the fact that his latest album hasn't been selling well.'

'And does Jane actually need to be there?'

'Need and want are two quite different things,' he said evenly. 'She says she does. Apparently the wear-and-tear factor is high. Julian gets through a whole load of stage clothes which she constantly needs to replenish. Though, as I told her, if he didn't insist on tipping bottles of champagne over his head and then diving all over the stage like a goalkeeper then maybe she wouldn't need to. She was out until the early hours last night—'

'But don't you *mind*?' asked Ursula breathlessly, the words tumbling out before she could stop them.

He raised his eyebrows at her, and Ursula was aware that she might have overstepped the line. Maybe he was regretting that illuminating glimpse into his marriage at Katy's party.

Today he was obviously attempting to be diplomatic about his wife's behaviour, she thought. And loyal.

'I'm an independent man who can survive my own company pretty well,' was all he said. 'But it's Katy's end-of-year production tonight, and Jane has promised she'll be back in time to watch her.'

'Oh.' Ursula bit back her indignation. It was all too easy for her to be critical of Jane's mothering and slightly in awe of Ross's quality as a father. Especially as she was bound to be biased in Ross's favour. And things were never that simple, that black and white—especially relationships. Why, even her sister and Finn—who loved each other to distraction—had had their ups and downs. 'I see. And why are you looking for a new cleaner?'

'Because Mrs Wilson walked out.'

'Really?'

'Really. The saxophone player from The Connection upset her. The guy with the diamond in his tongue—you remember?'

'He was pretty unforgettable,' said Ursula drily. 'How did he upset Mrs Wilson? Let me guess—beer on the carpet?'

'Not exactly,' Ross murmured drily. 'But after you'd left, he continued to drink like there was no tomorrow. He was pretty smashed by the end of it, and so he crashed out and spent the night on the sofa…' Ross's voice tailed off and he began to look as though he was regretting starting the conversation.

Ursula shrugged. 'So what was the problem with that? It's immature behaviour from a man of that age, but hardly a federal crime!'

'Except that he just happened to be naked.'

'Oh!' Ursula flashed him an innocent smile. 'But your cleaner has children of her own, doesn't she?'

'What's that got to do with anything?'

'Just that she's probably seen naked men before.'

'Yeah, she probably has, but in this case…'

Ursula frowned. 'In this case, what?'

He shook his head. 'It doesn't matter.'

'Of course it matters, Ross! You can't just start a conversation like that and then leave it hanging—'

'No.' And to Ursula's astonishment, Ross burst out laughing.

'*Now* what have I said that's so funny?' she demanded.

'Nothing. Just a rather unfortunate choice of word, that's

all!' He narrowed his eyes assessingly. 'I'd rather leave it, if you don't mind, Ursula.'

'Please tell me.'

He let out a sigh. 'Of course she had seen a naked man before!' he answered briskly. 'But in this case, what with it being first thing in the morning and everything...' He looked up, expecting embarrassed understanding in her eyes, but found nothing but confusion.

'Yes?' she prompted helpfully.

'Do I actually have to spell it out for you?'

'Yes, I think you do.'

Ross's frown deepened. 'Well, he was aroused.'

'He...was...aroused,' Ursula repeated slowly.

'Hell—yes! It was the *morning*, remember? And instead of just covering himself up—as anyone else might have done under the circumstances—he apparently gazed down at himself, then up at her and smirked and said, ''Hey, will you get a load of *that*, Mrs Wilson?'''

The true meaning of his words dawned on her, and Ursula went bright pink, her embarrassment made even worse by the way that Ross was staring at her, as if *he* had only just realised...

She might as well have got herself a huge placard and painted on it in bright, luminous capitals that she was completely innocent about what men's bodies did or didn't do first thing in the morning. Even simpler—why didn't she just wear a name badge bearing the single word 'Virgin!'?

'Oh, heck, Ursula,' he groaned. 'I didn't mean—'

'Please don't apologise, Ross,' she responded with dignity. 'You just weren't being terribly clear.'

'No, you're right,' he said slowly. 'I wasn't being terribly clear.'

Their eyes met in a long, defining moment. Ursula wondered whether he would opt for truth or concealment.

'Heck, Ursula,' he said again. 'I didn't realise—'

'That I was so ignorant in the ways of men?'

His eyes narrowed, the look in them one of dazed incredulity. 'Is that a roundabout way of saying that you're a...a—?'

She cut in before he could utter the damning word and embarrass the life out of both of them. 'I really don't think we should be having this conversation, Ross,' she told him steadily.

'No. No, of course not. Neither do I.' He heaved a sigh of relief, but his eyes were still curious. 'Then let's talk about something else.'

Ursula nodded. 'That might be best.'

There was a deafening and uncharacteristic silence.

Ross began to draw zigzagged lines in the margin of his notebook—always a sign that he was agitated. He lifted his head to look at her, those dark eyes glittering like jet—piercing, searching, questioning. She wanted to look away, but found that she couldn't.

And at that precise moment, to Ursula's everlasting relief, the telephone on her desk jangled into noisy life. She picked it up on the second ring. 'Ross Sheridan's office,' she said shakily.

It was a TV company which produced a daily audience participation programme. Ross had appeared on it once and had vowed never to set foot near the place again. Ursula dealt with the pushy researcher's request as efficiently and as politely as possible, aware all the time that Ross was sitting at his desk studying her, while pretending not to.

Great! She could just *imagine* what he was thinking.

Frumpy, unmarried *and* a virgin!

'Shall I go and buy a copy of the local paper?' she asked.

'To?'

'Look through the small ads for a replacement cleaner?'

He sighed. 'Would you, Ursula?'

'Or maybe it might just be better to arrange to have a bouquet of flowers delivered to Mrs Wilson, with a note saying it'll never happen again. That sort of thing?'

But he shook his head. 'Mrs Wilson seems to have already decided that the house is a den of iniquity.'

Ursula shrugged. 'Her loss.' But as she took a pound coin from the petty-cash tin she found herself wondering how Jane could be so stupid. Her face went pink again and she looked up.

'What?' said Ross.

Ursula shook her head. 'Nothing.'

'*What?*' he repeated impatiently.

'Well, it's a good thing it was only Mrs Wilson who went in there and saw him,' she ventured timidly. 'I mean, it might very well have been Katy.'

'Precisely,' he said, in a grim voice she had never heard him use before and at that moment her heart went out to him.

She went out to buy the newspaper and when she came back she trawled through the small ads and circled the likely candidates. 'Do you want me to ring round these numbers to try and find a new cleaner for you?' she asked Ross.

'Would you? Do you know what kind of thing to ask for?'

Ursula smiled. 'Why? Because I've never had to employ a cleaner in my whole life and probably never will?'

Ross shifted his long legs comfortably under the desk. 'Maybe.' He shrugged.

'Well, I know more than most people about professional cleaners,' she said. 'I know what is acceptable and what is not. It was a job my mother did for most of her adult life. I just hope you pay fair, Ross.'

A steady gaze was levelled at her. 'What do you think?'

She didn't hesitate. 'I'd hazard a guess that you probably pay over the odds.'

He smiled. 'Yeah.'

He began to draw tiny thumbnail sketches all over the margin of his notebook, and Ursula knew that the Sheridan brain was being bombarded with ideas for the latest campaign. The company was pitching for a new account—a hot new airline which everyone in the industry was hungry to represent. But Ross was putting together the package himself, and Ross would win the account—Ursula would have staked her entire month's salary on that!

The morning was taken up with meetings—first with Oliver Blackman, Ross's partner, who was flying off to Zurich at lunchtime. Next came Zara Hobbs, the new Accounts Director, who was blonde and beautiful, but just happened to be absolutely brilliant at her job. She also flirted like mad with Ross, Ursula noted in an objective sort of way. While Ross didn't even seem to notice…

After Zara, came an 'ideas' meeting with one of the other creative teams. This involved sitting around the large, round table and swopping ideas for a new beer campaign. A brainstorming session where, as usual, an interesting vision was given a defining twist of originality by Ross.

At one o'clock, they both went out for lunch with a client. The invitation had been for Ross and his partner, Oliver Blackman—but it had clashed with Oliver's trip to Switzerland. They went to a restaurant at the very top of a skyscraper with panoramic city views and a temperamental chef. Ursula had read about it in all the Sunday supplements, and it didn't disappoint.

The client was a dog-food manufacturer—not the kind of high-profile client Ross would normally have gone for—but, as he said to Ursula, he was a sucker for dogs! She

had often wondered why he didn't have one of his own—
she was sure Katy would love one—but he'd once told her
that Jane was allergic to dog hair.

Ross had masterminded the countrywide poster campaign, showing a smug-looking Labrador sitting with both
paws on a tin of dog food which was being marketed as
both cheap *and* nutritious. Everyone, Ursula included, had
teased the hell out of Ross for the corny line which had
accompanied the poster and had simply said, 'Paws For
Thought'. But Ross had argued that it was the dog's glo-
riously contented expression which would sell the brand.
'Just watch the sales figures,' he had predicted.

And the sales figures had said it all. As Oliver had remarked to Ursula—the man was just too clever for his own
good!

At four o'clock, when their one glass of lunchtime
Chablis was threatening to make them both doze off, Ursula
was just on her way out of the office in search of coffee
when the phone rang.

She turned immediately. 'I'll get it.'

'No, it's okay—I'll take it!' He stifled a yawn and lifted
up the phone. 'Hello?'

His body took on a sudden kind of tension as he listened
to the voice at the other end.

Instinct made Ursula remain rooted to the spot. Was it
bad news? she wondered as she saw the sudden stiffening
of his shoulders. Whatever the reason, she stayed there,
listening unashamedly—not because she was nosy, but because instinct told her that he might need her. And there
was no greater call to Ursula than that…

'I don't think I understand exactly what you mean,' Ross
was saying quietly into the telephone. He listened again for
a moment.

'Disappeared?' he demanded, his voice growing louder. 'What the hell are you talking about?'

He waited while the person at the other end said something else.

'Well, it's a pretty emotive word to use,' he said snarlingly. 'Particularly if you don't even know whether it's accurate or not!' His mouth twisted as the voice apparently tried to placate him, and he shook his dark head impatiently. 'No, please don't bother doing that. I'm on my way over.' He glanced at his watch. 'I'll be there as soon as it's humanly possible.'

There was a crash as he slammed the telephone back into its cradle and rose to his feet, his eyes unseeing, his face an odd, grey sort of colour.

From the door where she stood, Ursula gripped the handle. 'What's happened, Ross?' she croaked nervously. 'What's the matter?'

He focussed his eyes as though he had only just remembered that she was there, then fixed her with a piercing stare.

'Ross?' she prompted gently. 'What's happened?'

His words were slow and deep. He spoke as you would imagine a sleepwalker would speak. 'I have to go to the school to pick Katy up.'

'But what's happened?'

He gave a slight shake of his head, as if he had water in his ears and was trying to clear it. 'Jane was supposed to collect her...'

'And?'

'She hasn't turned up. The school say that she's disappeared.'

'What do they mean, she's "disappeared"?' Ursula demanded heatedly. 'Is she a missing person? Have they tried ringing her at home?'

'She sent a message via Julian's roadie—saying that she wouldn't be able to get to school, asking them to contact me. They said he—the roadie—sounded… I don't know… *strange*…'

Ursula tried to remain calm and sensible. She was a dab hand at handling bad news, but then she had a lifetime of experience to fall back on. 'Well, of course he would sound *strange*, Ross,' she said reasonably, 'if Jane had given him a message like that to leave. You'd hardly expect him to sound as though he was ringing up to see whether the school had a vacancy next term, would you?'

His eyes glittered like coal. 'I suppose not.'

'But why didn't Jane ring the school herself?' Ursula wondered softly.

'Right now I don't really *care*!' he emphasised savagely. 'All I care about is getting to Katy!'

He picked up his denim jacket with the air of a man ready to do battle.

'But you'll have to track her down,' said Ursula.

He stared at her, not seeming to have heard her.

'You'll have to trace her,' added Ursula gently. 'Jane, I mean. We don't live in the kind of society where someone can just disappear into thin air, do we?'

'That isn't my first priority. Nor even my second.' His eyes were hooded. 'Can you come with me, Ursula? Would you mind? Now?'

'*Me?*' she squeaked.

'Sure. Katy likes you—and there's no one better in a crisis. Plus, you once told me that you can cook,' he added flippantly.

She knew for a fact that he could, too—but she suspected that she wasn't being asked to accompany him for her culinary talents. Right now, her boss needed company. And help. Practical, female assistance.

'Of course I'll come,' she told him quietly.

'Then let's go!' he gritted, and strode out of the office.

CHAPTER FOUR

ALTHOUGH it was only just past four in the afternoon, the traffic was already beginning to build up—but then it was a hot Friday in July, and everyone except the tourists was rushing to get out of the middle of the city.

Ross and Ursula took a taxi all the way to North London, and it was getting on for five when the black cab slid to a halt in front of the large Victorian house which had been converted into a school.

A blind at one of the downstairs windows moved fractionally as the cab braked, and Ursula paid the driver while Ross leapt out of the car. She stuffed a couple of notes into the man's hand and then followed her boss inside, where the school secretary was waiting to meet them, her features compressed into a look of disapproval.

'Hello, Mr Sheridan,' she said primly.

'Where's my daughter?' he demanded immediately.

'She's in with the Head at the moment. She's—'

'Is she upset?'

The secretary looked hesitant. 'Not what I'd call *upset*. Obviously, she's a little worried—'

'Maybe that's because you adopted such a melodramatic attitude on the telephone!' suggested Ross, his dark brows winging upwards. 'Talking about Jane "disappearing" like that! I'm sure that there's a perfectly reasonable explanation for this.'

But his voice lacked its usual breezy conviction, and Ursula laid a gentle hand on his forearm. It wouldn't really help matters now if Ross started losing his temper. He needed Katy's school on his side—not against him. 'Please can we see Katy now?' she asked politely.

The school secretary looked Ursula up and down, clearly trying to place her in this whole scheme of things. Ursula could see the woman's genuine confusion—she certainly didn't look glamorous enough to be cast in the role of Ross's mistress, which, judging from the expression on the secretary's face, had been what she had been expecting!

'What—*both* of you?' the secretary asked.

Ursula shook her head. 'No. I'll wait here while you talk to Katy, Ross.'

'But I want you to come,' he argued stubbornly.

The secretary's mouth grew even thinner, and Ursula knew that her presence would only complicate matters. 'No. I'll wait for you here,' she repeated firmly.

He was gone for a little under fifteen minutes, and when he returned with a white-faced Katy at his side he looked mulish, and so did Katy, but neither of them said anything more than their rather stilted goodbyes until they were all outside again in the blistering July heat.

'Hello, Katy,' said Ursula softly.

Katy was studying her brown school sandals intently. ''Lo,' she said, without looking up.

Over her bent head Ursula looked at Ross and almost recoiled from the anger which was splintering from his dark eyes. But she was damned if she was going to wait to ask him any questions. Katy looked mixed up enough as it was. If they started clothing the whole situation in secrecy to spare her feelings then her childish imaginings would probably prove to be a whole lot worse than the truth itself.

Ursula found herself wondering just what the truth actually *was*. 'Any clues about where Jane's gone?' she asked bluntly.

'I don't think we need discuss that right now, do you?' came Ross's rather repressive reply.

Ursula ignored him, and bent down so that she was looking directly into Katy's eyes. 'When did you last see Mummy?'

Katy frowned as she tried to remember. 'Yesterday morning.'

'And did she say anything to you?'

'Like what?' asked Katy in bewilderment. 'She asked me what kind of cereal I wanted—the usual stuff.'

'And did she say anything about not coming to collect you from school this afternoon?' Ursula asked gently.

'The headmistress has already been through a hard-hitting interrogation,' said Ross caustically. 'And apparently has drawn a blank. She said that Katy wasn't very co-operative.'

But Ursula narrowed her deep blue eyes at him to warn him into silence. 'Then the headmistress clearly knows nothing!' she said briskly, and was rewarded with a small smile from the ten-year-old. 'Now, Katy—think back. Was there anything which made yesterday morning different from any other?'

Katy thought for a bit, then shrugged. 'I don't think so.' She thought for a moment again. 'Mummy was tired and grumbling a lot. She said she didn't know why Daddy couldn't have taken me into school and let her have a lie-in.'

'I just kind of assumed that she would want to take you herself,' said Ross evenly. 'As she hasn't done the school run much lately.'

Ursula could see that he was fighting like mad to control his temper. And she didn't blame him. 'Anything else, Katy?' she coaxed.

Katy shook her head and bit down on her lip, and when

she looked up at Ursula her eyes were swimming with tears. 'Just…just Julian,' she gulped eventually.

Ross stilled. 'What do you mean—just Julian?'

'We had to pick up Julian on the way to school—'

'What—you went over to Maida Vale?' queried Ross incredulously. 'At that time in the morning?'

Katy shook her head. 'He wasn't at his flat—he was staying in a hotel near *our* house.'

'Oh, *was* he?' asked Ross grimly. 'And why should that be, I wonder? Did Mummy say?'

'Ross, let's go home now,' said Ursula urgently, because she was afraid that he was going to say far too much in front of his daughter. At this stage nothing was certain, and presumptions about why Julian had been staying so close to the house would serve no purpose whatsoever. Especially if they turned out not to be true…

'The headmistress will be out in a moment,' she continued. 'And I've already seen the secretary peering out at us as though we're cluttering up the driveway. Come on— let's go.'

Ross looked about to argue with her, but something in the defeat suggested by Katy's slumped little shoulders seemed to change his mind. 'Okay,' he agreed. 'Let's go and find a cab.'

Ursula screwed her nose up at the suggestion. The journey over had been tense enough, with the two of them reluctant to start any meaningful conversations in front of the driver. And yet small talk at a time like this would be completely inappropriate. 'Who wants to sit in a stuffy car on an afternoon like this? Why don't we walk? It isn't very far, it's a lovely day, *and* there's an ice-cream van parked halfway down that road over there! What do you say?'

'Oh, *can* we, Daddy?' asked Katy, her face lighting for the first time since they'd arrived at the school.

Ross met Ursula's eyes. 'I guess so,' he murmured drily.

Soon the three of them were walking along Hampstead's wide, tree-lined roads, with Katy busy licking at a giant chocolate and cherry cornet. As a distraction technique the ice cream was perfect. Over the little girl's head, Ursula sent Ross a questioning look, but his eyes told her that he had no answers.

When they reached the house the three of them looked up at the window at the same time, as if fully expecting to see Jane Sheridan standing there, waiting for them.

But there was no sign of life.

'She might be inside,' said Ursula cheerfully, but neither Katy nor her father answered.

The house was completely empty—that much was obvious from the moment that Ross pushed the front door open—and they followed him in and stood in silence, listening. All that could be heard was the sound of the great grandfather clock ticking relentlessly away in the hall.

'I'd better go and take a look upstairs,' said Ross grimly, and the two females watched him take the stairs two at a time until he was out of sight.

Now what? thought Ursula. She saw the uncertainty on Katy's face and knew that the child needed some kind of distraction while the grown-ups attempted to come up with some answers. 'Tell you what, Katy.' She smiled. 'Why don't you go upstairs and get out of your school uniform? You look boiling in that blazer.'

'Can I take a bath?'

'Sure! Where do you want to take it?'

'Oh, ha ha!' giggled Katy, and the sound was like balm to Ursula's ears.

Ursula grinned. 'Of course you can! It's not often that a child *asks* for a bath!'

'Well, it's my end-of-year performance tonight,' confided Katy. 'And I play the springtime fairy—so I need my hair to be squeaky-clean. At least, that's what our drama teacher says, anyway!'

'Run along, then, kitten,' said Ross, appearing suddenly at the top of the stairs, and they both looked up at him, eyes wide with questions. He shook his head, and gave Katy a small, special smile.

'There's no letter from Mummy,' he said slowly, as he came down the stairs. 'But I expect she'll ring later to tell us what she's up to.'

Katy turned her big eyes up to gaze at her father. 'Will she, Daddy? Honestly?'

Ursula saw the shadows which played across his face and she knew he was wondering whether to tell the truth as he saw it, or keep a small girl's dream alive.

'I don't *know*, kitten,' he told her eventually. 'And that's the truth. But I'm sure she *will* get in touch. If only because of you. Because you know how much she loves you.'

'Yes,' said Katy dutifully, but couldn't keep the edge of doubt from her voice.

'Now what about that bath?' Ursula reminded her softly. 'Before your performance?'

'Okay!' said Katy, and she skipped away, actually looking quite *happy*.

'She doesn't seem too upset,' observed Ross thoughtfully as he watched her go.

And neither did he at that moment. 'That's kids for you,' she said. 'They can hurt like mad one minute, and be happily eating an ice cream the next. It's the short attention span.'

He nodded as he picked up a pile of mail from the telephone table, flipped through the stack of envelopes, then threw them back down again. 'And there's nothing there, either,' he growled.

'So now what?'

He shrugged his shoulders. 'How the hell should *I* know? It's not the kind of situation I have to deal with every day of my life!'

Ursula silently counted to ten—the man was clearly worried out of his head. But even so… 'You know, it's no good getting mad with *me*, Ross,' she told him quietly.

He raked an impatient hand back through the sudden wildness of his dark hair. 'No. You're right, of course. Getting angry won't solve anything. I just wish I knew what Jane was playing at right now!' His mouth twisted as he realised that his words could be taken two ways. 'Though maybe I've got a pretty good idea.'

Ursula stared at him in surprise. Even if the marriage had been rocky—which he had as good as admitted at Katy's party—he had still been married for over a decade. Surely he must feel *some* kind of sexual jealousy at the thought of Jane running off with Julian Stringer, a man known in the music business as 'sex on legs'?

But she was here to offer practical help, not to try and figure what was going on in that head of his.

'Shall I make you some tea?' she asked. 'Something to eat? Katy needs something before her performance. And while I'm cooking you can see whether you can track down Jane or not. Make a few phone calls. At least *do* something, Ross—don't just stand there glaring!'

The jet eyes glinted with reluctant admiration. 'How come you're never *quite* this bossy when we're in the office?'

She returned his gaze with a steady smile. 'Because in the office I work for you. Right now, I'm here as nothing but a friend. And even in times of trouble kids need to eat—*especially* in times of trouble! As do their daddies. So are omelettes okay for everyone?'

'Omelettes sound perfect.' He nodded, and just as she was about to turn away he reached out and caught her arm. Ursula's heart practically leapt out of her chest, the unexpected movement halting her in her tracks.

It was nothing more than the lightest of touches, and yet she could do nothing to stop the delicious shiver which catapulted its way up her spine. Her breath was caught in her throat. She couldn't remember ever being quite this close to him before, and—despite the circumstances which had brought her here—it was the most distracting experience of her life.

She found herself longing to nestle closer, to put her arms around his neck and hug him tightly, but knew she mustn't. *Mustn't.* His wife might have left him, but he was still a married man...

His eyes glittered, shadowed by a controlled anger which was only partially hidden by the dark, curving sweep of his lashes. She saw the unmistakable strain around his mouth, which had replaced his usual mocking smile with a grim twist of acceptance. He stared very hard at her, as if he was trying to look into her very soul. 'Why are you doing all this for me, Ursula?' he demanded rawly. 'What's in it for you?'

Her heart thundered even more. She was not going to rise to the sudden hostility in his voice. How could she *not* do it for him, when she cared for him so much? 'Because I like you, and I like Katy. Because you need a friend right now who will take you on any terms,' she told him very quietly. 'And I'm that friend.' She shrugged. 'That's all.'

He received this information in thoughtful silence. 'That's all?' he repeated, allowing his gaze to drift to the hand which was still resting on her arm, but he still didn't move it. 'Not many people would put themselves out the way you have. I think you underestimate yourself, Ursula.'

'D-do I?' she stumbled, disappointed and yet oddly relieved when he let the hand fall away. And she thought that Ross underestimated *himself*. She couldn't think of a single female who would turn down the opportunity to play guardian angel to Ross Sheridan and his daughter. She turned away. 'I'd better get started on those omelettes.'

'Sure.' His eyes followed her until she was almost by the kitchen door. 'Oh, Ursula?'

She spun round, surprising a look of unexpected softness on his face. 'Mmm?'

'Thanks,' he said simply.

How could a single word convey so much emotion? Somehow it was possibly the most affectionate thing he had ever said to her, and Ursula was awfully afraid she might do something stupid. Like sob. Or fling comforting arms around him. Or tell him that she'd walk to the ends of the earth and back if he asked her to!

Time to get out of here!

'I'll start making dinner,' she announced briskly, and pushed open the swing door into the kitchen.

CHAPTER FIVE

URSULA was glad she had opted for something simple like eggs to cook—because Ross and Jane's kitchen certainly didn't run to the exotic. Or even to most of the essentials. It was a room designed by someone who obviously liked style, but not cooking. There were lots and lots of gadgets—upmarket nutcrackers and a gleamingly expensive chrome expresso maker. But the stock cupboard was bare except for the basics—salt, pepper, vinegar and a couple of bottles of sauce.

She had to use Cheddar cheese instead of Parmesan for the omelette, and there was no fancy balsamic vinegar to add zing to her French dressing. But she did find a French stick in the freezer which only needed ten minutes in the oven to transform the room with its delicious smell.

Ross came in with Katy just as she was sliding the last omelette on the plate, and Ursula looked up at him, a question in her eyes, but he shook his head and said nothing.

Which she guessed meant that he was no nearer to finding out where Jane had gone.

Katy's hair was still damp, and she looked bewildered as she sat down at the window table opposite her father.

'Have some bread,' said Ursula gently, and pushed the warm bread towards her.

'I'm not hungry,' mumbled Katy.

'But you *must* be hungry, kitten,' argued Ross. 'That ice cream can't have filled you up.'

'And you've got a performance to get through tonight,'

Ursula reminded her. 'Just eat up a little bit, and see how you go.'

'You need more than just a bit—' Ross began to growl, but Ursula fixed him with a look of warning designed to shut him up—a message he clearly understood, since he raised his eyebrows with an air of mockery and began to pile a great spoonful of green salad onto his plate.

Without any pressure, Katy ate over half her meal, which was more than Ursula had thought she would manage, and then asked to be excused to get ready for the play.

'We need to leave at seven, Daddy.'

Ross tore off a chunk of bread. 'Okay.'

Katy hesitated by the door. 'And can…can Ursula come, too?'

'Of course she can.' Ross stared deep into Ursula's sapphire eyes. 'But she may be busy,' he answered evenly, his expression telling Ursula that here was her opportunity to leave if she wanted to.

'No, I'm not busy,' she answered immediately, not caring whether that made her look lonely and desperate. The child was miserable and missing her mother, and seemed to want *her* support—now was not the time to play stupid games to try and make it appear to Ross that her social life was sparkling! 'Thank you for asking me, Katy. I'd absolutely love to come!'

'Good!' Katy flashed her a grateful smile. 'I'll go and get ready, then!'

There was a brief silence after she had gone. Ross wiped his mouth with his napkin and then leaned back in his chair and studied Ursula across the table.

'You're pretty good at coaxing little girls to eat,' he remarked.

Ursula pushed her plate away. 'That's not surprising, really. My sister used to need a fair bit of persuasion, too.

It's natural not to want to eat when you're unhappy. Or sleep. Or do most, things, actually. Normal life is the hardest thing to achieve if you're aching inside.'

He nodded slowly and seemed about to say something on the subject of unhappiness, but asked instead, 'How about some coffee?'

'Okay.' Ursula respected his need to focus on the mundane—in times of crisis it could be the only thing which kept you sane. Cups of coffee were easier to think about than where his wife might have gone. He looked white with worry and fatigue. 'I'll make some,' she said, moving to rise from her chair, but Ross stopped her with an irritable shake of his head.

'No, sit down. *I'll* make the coffee, Ursula,' he told her tetchily. 'You cooked the meal, and we're not at work now. Are we?' He flashed her a look of pure challenge as he rose to his feet, towering over her in a way which was making her feel almost delicate. His mouth hardened. 'Or have you slotted me into the hopeless chauvinist category— the kind of man who can't cope in a kitchen? Or *won't* cope in a kitchen if there happens to be a woman around?'

Ursula laughed, amused by his overreaction. 'Skip the lecture on equality, Ross!' she teased him gently. 'I'd love a coffee—and I don't have the slightest problem with you making it! Shall I stack the plates in the dishwasher while you're making it, or would you rather do *that* yourself?'

'Stack away.' He smiled thinly.

He was just reaching out towards the kettle when she heard him make a muffled exclamation beneath his breath. Ursula glanced up from the dishwasher to see him pulling out a white envelope from where it stood propped at the back of the coffee jar.

That'll be from Jane, she thought, feeling her pulse begin to rocket, but she didn't say a word as she watched Ross

rip the envelope open and then pull out the single sheet of
typewritten paper which was inside, his eyes scouring it
rapidly, like a speed reader.

She carried on methodically stacking the dishes, then
wiped stray crumbs off the table and prayed that Katy
wouldn't come in for a minute or two—or at least until
Ross had had time to compose himself. Ursula didn't dare
look at him—she didn't know if she could cope with seeing
his heartbreak—and seconds ticked by excruciatingly.

'She's gone,' said Ross baldly, as he balled the sheet of
paper within his large fist and tossed it disdainfully down
onto the work surface.

She dared meet his eyes at last, reading bitterness and
anger there. But no regret. Maybe that would come later,
she thought, once the initial shock had passed.

'It's from Jane?' she said dully, because it was the kind
of situation where the obvious kept being stated—maybe
as a way of drumming in the hard facts.

He nodded. 'Yeah,' he drawled with distaste, as if the
word had been contaminated. 'It's from Jane.'

Trying to keep her face impartial, Ursula merely nodded.
'And does she say where she's gone?'

'Not precisely. Here—read it!' And he picked up the
crumpled ball of paper and threw it to her.

Ursula caught it with a protest. 'I can't read this, Ross!'

'But I want you to,' he said stubbornly. 'Go on—*read*
it!'

She was woman enough and curious enough to protest
no more, and Ursula smoothed the crumpled letter out onto
the table. It was addressed only to Ross, she noted—not
Katy. She read:

Dear Ross,
By the time you read this—I will be gone. (Oh, God—

did I *really* write that? Why do major life events always have to sound so corny and predictable?!)

Ursula flinched and stole a brief glance at Ross, but he was standing in front of the kitchen window staring out at the golden beauty of the summer evening. He was perfectly still—so still that he might have been carved from stone, his whole body frozen into immobility. A muscle flickering in one cheek was the only outward sign that anything was wrong.

Ursula carried on reading.

I am sure that my departure will come as no great shock to you (except, perhaps, for its suddenness), since we both know that things haven't been good between us for a while now. Or could that classify as an understatement? Yes, I think it probably could!

Ursula's heart picked up speed, and she was appalled to acknowledge that those last few flippant words had given her some kind of gruesome *pleasure*. How could she? How *could* she delight in the fact that their marriage had been in tatters? She swallowed down her guilt and continued.

I need some space, Ross—and yes, I can see you screwing your face up with distaste as you read those words, but I can't help it if you seem to have a problem with commonplace phrases which everyone else uses except you.

I'm going to Australia, with Julian, but it's too early to say whether my relationship with him will grow into something more than it is at the moment. Whatever happens, I'll contact you from there.

Please send Katy all my love, and tell her that I'm

sorry. That everyone only gets one shot at life, and that one day she may understand why I had to do this.

Yours, Jane.

Ursula's fingers were trembling as she held the letter out towards him. 'Here—'

'I don't want it!' he snarled.

'Then destroy it!' she urged. 'Unless, of course, you want Katy to see it?'

His laugh was cold and cynical. 'What? And show her that she rated a nothing more than a couple of brief sentences right at the end of her mother's *letter*?' He spat the last word out with contempt.

'A lot of men might have been tempted to show her for *precisely* that reason,' observed Ursula quietly.

'What? To demonstrate what a bitch my wife can be, and hurt my daughter even more in the process?' Ross's dark eyes glittered. 'I may be feeling pretty angry, Ursula, but I'm not into scoring cheap points like *that*!'

Now he seemed to be attacking *her*! But Ursula recognised that he needed someone to lash out at right now, someone who wouldn't take it personally…and that someone happened to be her. 'I wasn't for a moment suggesting that you were,' she responded calmly. 'You're a good man, Ross. And a good father.'

'You can't possibly know that!' he snarled.

'Oh, yes, I can,' she contradicted, meeting his blazing eyes with confidence. 'I know the first part, certainly—I've worked with you long enough to judge that for myself. The second part I can only base on the times I've seen you with Katy, and the way you interact with each other—there's no hiding the love she obviously feels for you.'

'Thanks.' He closed his eyes with something approaching despair. 'But I'm no saint, Ursula,' he whispered suddenly. 'Don't ever think that.'

Her throat constricted. Were a thousand fantasies about her perfect man about to crumble to dust? 'Are you trying to say that you were unfaithful to Jane?' she whispered.

He shook his head. 'Never.' The denial was too swift and too emphatic to be anything other than the truth. And then his eyes glittered again. 'Perhaps I've been guilty of impure thoughts from time to time, but nothing more than that.'

'And Jane?' she asked quietly.

'Our relationship may have been spiralling into freefall,' he observed caustically, 'but I'm not the kind of man to be cuckolded, least of all by the mother of my child.'

No. Ursula winced. This was more painful than she had expected. Yet something drove her on to expose herself to even more pain. 'But how can you be so sure about that, Ross?'

He looked at her assessingly, as if wondering just how frank to be. 'Because I know my wife,' he said slowly. 'I know her moods…and her body language. Believe me when I tell you that she was never unfaithful to me. Until now.' He paused. 'That's why she's gone. Because she can't look me in the eye any more. She's fallen in love. I knew it would happen eventually. It was just a question of waiting.'

'But don't you *mind*?' she asked breathlessly, because part of him sounded almost *glad* about it.

His smile was cynical. 'When something is dead, you can't bring it back to life,' he said flatly. 'But she shouldn't have left that way. Her behaviour has been that of a child, not a woman and a mother. For Katy's sake, she could have handled it better.'

'But how on earth could she have done that?'

'We had an understanding,' he said simply. 'Based on honesty.'

It struck Ursula that it was an old-fashioned word to use. And that she had no right to ask him exactly what that understanding had been.

'She knew how important the truth was to me,' he said quietly. 'Yet she chose a devious way of getting what she wanted. Running away like a fugitive,' he added in disgust. 'And deceit like that has the power to destroy what little harmony remained between us. I didn't want that to happen. For Katy's sake.'

'But how did it all go so wrong, Ross?' she questioned. 'Was it because you married so young?'

He shook his head. 'We were both twenty-one. Not infants. No one held a gun at my head.' He gave a low, cruel laugh. 'Though maybe in a way, they did.'

She tried to imagine him getting married at twenty-one. It was a mental image which stubbornly refused to appear. Maybe because it made her heart turn over with jealousy. She had seen a photo of him at that age and he had looked impossibly young and unimaginably beautiful. 'It must have been a grand passion,' she observed quietly.

His gaze mocked her. 'Don't play games with me, Ursula—'

'I'm not—'

'You must have been able to work out from the time-scale involved that Jane was pregnant with Katy when we got married.'

'Well, then,' said Ursula triumphantly. 'It *must* have been a grand passion, mustn't it, for you to have taken risks like that? Or did you just not take contraception into account?'

He looked at her steadily. 'I presume that's meant to be a criticism?'

She shook her head. 'I didn't mean it to be. I was just brought up to believe that sex was too important not to think about the consequences.'

Ross's eyes widened by a fraction, as though he couldn't quite believe what she had just said. 'Do you know, I can't decide which I find the more endearing quality—your total innocence or your touching faith in human nature!'

'Don't make fun of me.'

'I'm not. Really, I'm not. I admire your morality, if you really want to know. And I'm just trying to find a practical solution to this whole damned situation. The best way forward for Katy.'

'You could always get another au pair?'

He shook his head. 'No, I couldn't. I don't want to bring a stranger in to care for Katy—not at a time like this. A young girl with no experience of children—keener on having a good time than dealing with a child who may be troubled.'

'No, I suppose not.'

He paused and watched her, as a cat would a mouse, until his silent scrutiny compelled her to look directly into the dark, glittering vortex of his eyes. 'Would you help me, Ursula?' he asked her deliberately.

She was genuinely confused. 'Help you with what?'

'Help me with Katy—'

'Ross, I don't know anything about young girls—'

'Yes, you do,' he contradicted. 'You have a younger sister.'

'But Amber's grown up now!'

'But she wasn't always, was she? And you virtually brought her up single-handed when your mother was sick—you told me that yourself. And little girls don't change that much. Not fundamentally.' He stared at her from between narrowed eyes.

Ursula lifted her fingertips to one rather flushed cheek, and fleetingly thought what a mess she must look. 'What exactly are you asking me, Ross? That I give up my job in order to care for Katy? Because she's going to need someone here when she gets home from school and during the holidays. And the summer holiday starts very soon. Unless...' She hesitated, unable to keep the horror from her face. 'Unless you're planning to send her away to boarding-school?'

'Never, ever.' He shuddered. 'And the last thing I want is for you to give up your job—I'm far too selfish for that. We've worked together for so long I can't imagine life without you.'

I wish he wouldn't *say* things like that, thought Ursula fiercely. Doesn't he know how stupid compliments like that could turn a woman's head? Especially a woman who isn't used to receiving them. But she kept her expression deadpan. 'What, then?'

'We could easily arrange to work *here*, so that there's always someone here to greet Katy.'

Ursula blinked. 'Just like that?'

'Why not? I'm the boss—well, Oliver is, too—and the creative side of the business is what I do best, and I work best where I'm happy. And I'll be most happy if I know that my daughter doesn't have an empty house to come home to. Think about it, Ursula. Term-times will be easy. We already schedule most meetings for the mornings. What do we do in Soho that we couldn't do right here? And I'm only talking from three until six every day.'

Ursula frowned. 'Well, I suppose when you put it like that...'

'School holidays will obviously take a bit of planning—but we could work it out between us, surely?'

Ursula nodded. 'I can't see too many problems with that. Lots of people are away during school holidays.'

Those dark eyes of his looked so appealing…? Almost too appealing, really, and suspicion entered Ursula's heart. She gazed at him sceptically as her thoughts slotted themselves into some kind of pattern. 'This isn't the first time you've thought of this brilliant idea, is it, Ross?' she said slowly.

Wariness replaced appeal. His eyes narrowed. 'What do you mean?'

'Well, it hasn't just come to you out of the blue, has it? It's much too well thought out to be a sudden brainwave,' she challenged. 'Even for you. And, now that I come to think of it, you've been making odd remarks and asking unusual questions over the last few weeks—'

'Like what?'

'Like, "Ursula, do you *like* working in the centre of London?" and "Ursula, have you ever felt like changing your job?"' His eyes looked almost black as she stared at him. 'Did you know that Jane was going to leave you?'

There was an odd kind of silence. 'No,' he said eventually. 'Not exactly. But I sensed that the situation was building up towards some sort of crisis.'

Ursula stared at him. 'Well, why the hell didn't you come right out and ask her about it, instead of letting it reach this kind of situation?'

For the first time since they'd arrived back, he snapped. 'Oh, no, Ursula!' He shook his head in denial. 'Don't try and use your obvious inexperience to offer me advice on what I *should* have done—'

How *dare* he throw her inexperience back in her face? 'I don't have to stay here if you're going to insult me, you know!'

'No, I know you don't,' he answered back. 'Just trust

me when I tell you that sometimes the best thing you can do is just sit back and let things happen. Even if something at the very heart of you screams out that it's all wrong.' His face was etched with pain. 'That whenever there is a child involved the status quo, however unsatisfactory, seems preferable to ripping apart the very fabric of that child's life.' He looked at her. 'Do you understand what I'm saying?'

She nodded. 'I think so.'

'I was in a bad marriage where we'd lost the ability to communicate a long time ago. If I'd challenged Jane simply to save face, I'd have risked losing Katy. And it simply wasn't worth it.'

Ursula stared at him in astonishment, as if he had just announced that he had spent most of his formative years in jail! 'But you never said anything to me, Ross! You've never mentioned a *word* about this before! You used to come into work, day after day, always with a smile on your face. I would never have guessed that anything was so wrong in your life!'

He gave an odd kind of smile. 'What's to say? What would be the point of coming into the office saying, ''Morning, Ursula—oh, by the way, did I ever tell you that my marriage is in one hell of a mess?''?'

He regarded her steadily. 'And, to be honest, I wanted to keep my marriage completely separate from my job. The office became like a kind of sanctuary. Work has always fulfilled me—that and seeing Katy grow up. And you were always so steady and so sweet and so funny. Like a balm to my raw senses. I actually looked forward to coming in each morning.'

Ursula's heart resumed its thundering, but she forced herself to take his words at face value, not to read anything else into them. He had flattered her by revealing that he found her easy and comforting company in the midst of his personal crisis, but that was all. 'Then why didn't you *do* something about it sooner?' she questioned. 'Why let something bad drag on and on?'

'If you mean divorce then the reasons are the same as the ones I've just given you.'

'No!' she denied defensively, firmly telling herself that divorce had been the furthest thing from her mind. Definitely. 'I didn't mean divorce. I meant reconciliation. Counselling. Or something.' She shrugged. 'Whatever it is that people do these days. I don't know! I've never been married.'

'No.' He shrugged. 'Some options we had already explored. Unsuccessfully—as you've probably guessed.'

She saw the strain intensified on his face, and realised that Katy would be back any minute. And she owed Ross more than this frosty kind of questioning.

Much more.

'Yes, I'll help you with Katy,' she told him softly. 'Of course I will. And I'll do whatever it takes to ease the pain, and confusion.'

Some of the tension around his mouth eased, and the look of gratitude he gave her made her feel as mushy as a soft-centred chocolate.

'But there's just one thing I want you to promise me, Ross,' she said.

'Name it.'

'I don't want my sister to know anything about this arrangement we've made.'

He frowned. 'But I hardly ever see Amber, do I?'

'No, but you run across Finn from time to time, and sometimes you speak to Amber when she phones me. I'd rather they didn't know that I was going to help you with Katy. Not just yet, anyway. I'll tell her in my own time.'

His dark gaze was piercing. 'Any particular reason?'

Ursula felt uncomfortable as his bright stare lanced through her defences. 'They think I work hard enough as it is,' she said. 'That's all.'

But Ross was not easily fobbed off with lame excuses. The dark eyes remained quizzical for a moment, before comprehension dawned in them with a raw black gleam. 'Oh, I think I understand,' he said slowly. 'They're protecting you. They won't want you getting involved with a married man?'

'But I won't be *getting* involved with a married man, will I?' she questioned patiently, though the blood was pounding in her head. 'I'm just helping you with your daughter.'

His gaze was mocking. 'And you think you can do one without the other happening?'

She considered this. 'I think so.'

He nodded. 'How can I ever thank you?' he queried, very softly.

Ursula almost suggested a good way would be by taking her in his arms and hugging her—simply as a friend, of course. But that was out of the question. Because in Ross's eyes she was nothing more than Good Old Ursula, his plump, reliable assistant—as comfortable and as unexciting as an old pair of slippers.

And not only did men like Ross Sheridan never fall for women like that.

It seemed that they never hugged them either...

CHAPTER SIX

December

KATY'S lips curled into a near-perfect pout as she stared at her father. 'But, Daddy—*why*? Why can't Ursula spend Christmas Day with us?'

Across the sitting room of his Hampstead home, Ross threw Ursula a look, the kind of look which said, 'Over to you, O'Neil'! And he kept that infuriating half-smile pinned to his lips as he answered his daughter's question with an evasive, 'I don't know exactly, kitten—why don't you ask her?'

'Why, Ursula?' repeated Katy quietly, a determined and intent look on her face.

Without missing a beat, Ursula continued to unload scarlet and gold wrapped presents from the bulging carrier bag she had brought in with her. 'Because I have to spend Christmas Day with my sister, Amber,' she replied steadily, as she carefully placed the gifts beneath the Christmas tree which she and Katy had decorated. 'I already explained that.'

'But you've only just come *back* from a holiday!' objected Katy moodily. 'When you went looking for that wedding dress!'

'You don't begrudge me a holiday, surely?' asked Ursula, laughing.

The pout disappeared, and Katy set her mouth into a stubborn line which made her look the image of her father.

'But you *always* spend Christmas Day with your sister!' she observed.

'Exactly!' said Ursula triumphantly. 'So she'd think it pretty odd if I didn't this year, wouldn't she?'

'Well, why can't you just tell her that you want to spend it with Daddy and me for a change?' pleaded Katy. 'Because you *do* want to spend Christmas with us, don't you, Ursula?'

Ursula sighed, fixing Ross with a 'rescue me' expression, but he completely ignored it. Just continued his policy of pleasant non-cooperation—with nothing more than a slightly shrugged look of bemusement. Awkward beast!

Ursula sent him a half-hearted frown. 'Of *course* I want to spend Christmas Day with you and D...your daddy,' she amended with a sigh. 'But I see you nearly all the time as it is, and Amber is the only family I've got, and—'

'But Daddy says your sister's engaged now!' Katy pointed out slyly. 'To the man who owns the model agency.'

'To Finn. Yes, she is.' Ursula's head shot up sharply. 'So?'

Katy ignored her father's warning look. 'So—won't they want to be on their own? So they can get all lovey-dovey, and stuff like that! Won't you be a gooseberry if you hang around?'

'Why? Is that what *Daddy* told you?' questioned Ursula sweetly, the look she directed at Ross lit with the light of battle.

'Why don't you run upstairs and get ready for bed now, Katy?' suggested Ross hastily. 'Because the sooner you go to sleep—'

'"The sooner Christmas Day will come!"' chimed Katy obediently. 'Okay.' She moved over to where her father was sprawled in one of the armchairs, looking like a man who didn't know how to relax properly. She bent and kissed the top of his dark, wavy head. 'You need a haircut, Daddy,' she remarked.

Ross laughed up at her. 'That's neat—coming from a ten-year-old who has to be dragged screaming to the hairdresser's!'

'Oh, *I* didn't say you needed it!' said Katy airily. 'Ursula did!'

'Oh, did she?' queried Ross softly, and now the light of battle was in *his* eyes.

Ursula averted her gaze. She didn't feel like looking at him just now. Instead, she raised her arms up as Katy came over and gave her a big hug and a kiss. 'I'll come and say goodnight and wish you a happy Christmas before I go,' she told the child.

'And when will we see you?' asked Katy breathlessly.

Ursula stroked a whirly strand of hair off Katy's cheek, deciding that she would not let her irritation with Ross affect her relationship with his daughter. 'I could come straight round here tomorrow night, when I get back from Amber and Finn's place—if it's early enough. How about that?'

'*Could* you? That would be perfect!' murmured Katy, nuzzling her nose into Ursula's neck, like a little puppy dog.

'*And* I'm coming to Prague with you and Daddy next week, don't forget!' Ursula reminded her. 'Just think of the New Year's Eve we'll have!'

'With Mummy,' Katy put in hesitantly.

'That's right,' said Ursula evenly. 'Mummy will be there, too—'

'And Julian.'

'And Julian,' echoed Ursula, and this time she didn't

have to look pleadingly at Ross for him to leap in smoothly to her assistance.

'Off you go to bed now, kitten.' He smiled, his face betraying nothing of the conflict of emotions which Ursula knew the forthcoming trip to Prague had stirred up. 'Or Father Christmas won't come down the chimney later!'

Father's and daughter's eyes met.

'Oh, *Daddy*!'

'What?' he replied innocently.

'*You* know!' Katy twinkled.

Ross shrugged. 'All *I* know is that if you don't believe in him, he won't come. It's as simple as that! Even for grown-ups. Believing is everything. Okay?'

Ursula recognised the blinding relief in Katy's smile, knowing that this year—of all years—she needed to hold onto her dreams. After all, it wasn't every year that your mother left without saying a proper goodbye. Then phoned you only intermittently from around the other side of the world. Or sent presents which were supposed to compensate but never really did, no matter how expensive they were. Katy was a brave little girl, Ursula thought with a pang.

'Okay, Daddy! I'll go upstairs and get straight to sleep!' And Katy skipped from the room with a last, fleeting smile.

There was silence after she had gone, and Ursula felt Ross's eyes on her—though it was a moment or two before she could meet them with any degree of calm.

'Katy seems…okay,' she observed. 'I'd been wondering if she'd find it extra difficult—being Christmas and all that.'

'Yes, she does.' But his eyes looked bitter. 'Jane rang at lunchtime today.'

'Christmas Eve *lunchtime*?' Ursula blinked. 'Bit of an

odd time to ring. Why didn't she ring this evening—before Katy hung her stocking up?'

'It's the time difference in Australia,' he explained evenly. 'She was just going to bed.'

'Oh.' Maybe it was best not to dwell on Jane's sleeping habits. Ursula bent to pick up a discarded sweet wrapper instead.

'I wish you weren't going to Amber's,' he said suddenly, and she straightened up to find him staring at her.

Ursula had learnt to guard against the odd crumb of af-fection which Ross occasionally threw her way. She had decided that it didn't actually mean anything, and just com-plicated what was a very workable arrangement.

Because, in the five months since Jane Sheridan had left the family home and gone off to live in Australia, Ursula had become indispensable to Ross and Jane. She knew that. They knew that. And it suited them all.

But only for the time being! She kept having to remind herself of that. Only until Ross and Jane had sorted out their situation one way or another. Or until *she* met a man whom she could settle down with.

Ursula stifled a sigh. If only she could be bothered!

At the moment it just seemed so unlikely. Especially when such close contact with Ross only rubbed in just how *lacking* other men were—in just about every department which mattered.

For the first time ever, she was beginning to be a bit of a clock-watcher, and always tried to go home bang on the dot of six—simply because, as she kept telling Ross, it was important that he spent some one-to-one time with his daughter. Though—if she were being truthful—she was acting on a purely self-protective instinct. Too much ex-posure to Ross at home was madness!

But Katy always wanted her to stay. More to the point—

so did Ursula! It was usually left to Ross to be the calm, noncommittal member of the trio, who didn't seem to care one way or another whether she lingered or not.

But not tonight, it seemed.

Now he seemed to be renewing his attack.

'So can't you stay for Christmas Day?' he persisted. 'Really?'

Ursula tried to fill her voice with conviction. 'Oh, yeah, sure! I can just imagine how pleased my sister would be if I told her that I'd changed my mind—especially after she's been out and bought a mountain of sprouts and an aeroplane-sized turkey!'

'She probably *wouldn't* care, if you stopped to think about it. Maybe she'd prefer to spend the day in bed with Finn,' he suggested deliberately. 'Alone.'

Ursula felt far too anxious to be embarrassed by his sexy statement. She shook her head so emphatically that her hair swung wildly round her neck, like frayed black satin. 'That's just where you're wrong,' she told him worriedly. 'I don't think that the two of them have been getting along too well just lately.'

Ross pleated his mouth into a disapproving line. 'I can't say I'm particularly surprised—'

'And what's that supposed to mean?'

Ross shrugged. 'Well, I like your sister very much—but I can't blame Finn for being angry with her. I mean—whatever possessed her to give that dreadful interview to '*Wow!*' magazine?'

Loyalty came naturally to Ursula. 'Oh, come on—it wasn't *that* dreadful!' she defended, even though the piece in question had caused her to cringe with embarrassment when she had read it.

'Sure it was! It was worse than dreadful! Amber was sprawled out looking unbelievably sexy in about eight different shots *and* she was blabbing about her relationship with Finn!' He shook his head rather sorrowfully. 'Without even bothering to tell him that she'd done the interview! You can't really blame Finn for blowing his top—*I'd* have been pretty angry if it had been me!'

Privately, Ursula agreed with Ross. But it was one thing criticising your *own* flesh and blood—quite another matter if somebody else had the cheek to do it!

'She hardly gave away any state secrets, did she?' disagreed Ursula doggedly.

'Well, she told the world how Finn had proposed to her—and did it in such a way that everyone could tell that he'd done it straight after having sex with her—'

'Ross!'

'But it's true.'

Ursula frowned, her concern for her sister making her oblivious to the fact that she was discussing sex with her boss! 'I know,' she sighed. 'Which is why it's extra important that I spend Christmas Day with them—maybe I can stop them from killing one another!'

He glanced up at her, his dark eyes narrowing critically. 'You look tired.'

'I am, a bit.'

'So break the habit of a lifetime. Stay and have a drink.'

It was tempting… She shook her head. 'No, really— I ought to get home and wrap Amber and Finn's presents—'

'Oh, that!' he scoffed. 'That won't take long, surely? Stay and have a drink with me, Ursula—I haven't seen you for almost a fortnight.' He stood up and went over to the drinks cabinet where he opened a bottle of claret and poured them both a glass. 'Since you took your impromptu little holiday—'

'So now *you're* objecting as well as Katy, are you?'

He shook his head, and gave a tight smile as he handed

her a glass of wine. 'Of course I'm not objecting! It's just that I...we...well, we missed you... That's all. Especially Katy.'

'Yes,' answered Ursula slowly. She sank down onto one of the squashy sofas and sipped her drink. 'I missed her, too.' And her daddy.

Ross sat down opposite her. 'So what's all this about a wedding dress?'

Ursula had let her eyelids drift down; now she opened them again and looked at him. 'Mmm?'

'Katy mentioned it just a minute ago. Something about you going off to find a wedding dress.'

'Oh!' Ursula wrinkled her nose. 'It isn't really a story designed to appeal to men—'

'Don't patronise me, Ursula,' he warned softly.

Across the room, their eyes clashed and Ursula's heart beat out a frantic and erratic beat. 'I wouldn't dream of patronising you.'

'I want you to tell me the story,' he told her stubbornly.

Ursula's mouth twitched. 'Oh, do you?'

He captured her gaze and didn't look away as he murmured, 'Yes, I do.'

She swirled the claret around in the crystal glass and the ruby light bounced and dazzled off her fingers. 'You remember I told you that my mother worked as a cleaner, when I was a child?'

He nodded. 'Along with giving me a stern lecture about not exploiting *my* cleaner!'

'Did I?' She sipped her drink again, and the wine gave her courage. 'Well, she cleaned in a big department store because we were extremely poor,' she added baldly.

Ross hid a gentle smile. 'I was able to draw my own conclusions,' he remarked. 'I didn't imagine that she was doing a job like that out of the goodness of her heart—or

because she opted for low wages, or because she wanted
to observe human behaviour! So what happened?'

Ursula's eyes became wistful. 'My mother was an in-
curable romantic who fell in love with a designer wedding
dress. She saved up and queued up all night, and bought it
in the sale—'

'And was it beautiful?' he interrupted. 'This dress?'

'Oh, it was exquisite.' She read the question in his eyes.
'No, of course it wasn't for *her*—she was already married!
It was for us—her two daughters to wear. Me first, and
then Amber.' She laughed, but it was tinged with a slightly
brittle sound. 'Except that Amber's getting married before
me—of course!'

He completely ignored the self-deprecating remark. 'So
what became of the dress?'

'My father became sick, and then he died—'

His face softened. 'Yes. I'm sorry.'

'Thank you.' She sipped her drink and swallowed down
her sadness. 'After his death we were even more broke than
before, and my mother was forced to sell the dress. No one
has seen it since…'

Ross studied her with interest. 'So the trail went cold,
did it?'

'Kind of.' Ursula nodded. 'But then—quite by chance—
I happened to see a competition in a newspaper. The daughter of the original designer has made a replica of the dress,
and she's raffling the gown in the New Year to publicise
the opening of her new shop. So I've entered Amber's
name in the competition to win it!'

'But not your own?'

She was angry that he had been insensitive enough to
ask the question, because now she would have to answer
him in shaming detail. '*I'm* not the one getting married,

Ross—and even if I were I'm much too fat to wear the dress!'

He screwed his eyes up as he looked at her—the way he did when he was working and trying to visualise how a finished advertisement would look on the page of a magazine. 'Are you?' he asked, as though her shape wasn't important, and something in the way he said it filled her with fury.

'It's a tiny size, and a narrow, fitted design!' she snapped. 'So *of course* I'm too fat to wear it!'

'You sound angry, Ursula,' he commented mildly. 'Surely not because your sister is thinner than you?'

Yes, she *was* angry, and no—it *wasn't* because Amber had the more fashionable figure. This anger was of the bubbling away variety, the type which was rapidly coming to the boil. Had part of her hoped that, with Jane settled with her lover on the opposite side of the world, her platonic relationship with Ross would be rebuilt into one of intimacy?

Why hadn't Ross ever noticed her shape before? Not because he was still legally married, that was for sure—but because he regarded her less as a woman, and more as part of the fixtures and fittings. Suddenly, Ursula felt shackled by her comfortable shape and her comfortable image.

'Let's skip it, shall we?' she questioned sulkily.

Ross continued to regard her steadily, and Ursula could tell from that determined expression that he had no intention of skipping it. 'So why didn't you tell me this intriguing little story before?'

'Because usually men aren't interested in weddings or their spin-off products!' she told him heatedly. 'Traditionally, they run a mile if the subject is brought up! And even if I had thought you *were* interested—it wasn't the most diplomatic of topics to bring up, was it? I didn't think that you'd want to hear anything about matrimony, considering...'

There was a split-second pause. Ross raised his eyebrows. 'Considering what?'

Well, she couldn't chicken out now. Facing facts was what grown-ups had to do. 'Considering your wife left you less than six months ago.'

'Oh, she left me a long time before that,' he said, in a voice so low she could barely hear him.

She wanted to ask him, to quiz him—to find out what had *really* gone so desperately wrong with his marriage. But part of her also wanted his secrets to remain just that. She didn't need the added complication of sharing his pain, because his personal life was not her territory.

And, in any case, Christmas Eve was not the time to talk about failed relationships...

Ursula put her empty glass down on the coffee table and stood up. 'Time I was going, I think.'

Ross levered himself off the sofa, and as he moved towards her she caught the faintest trace of lemon and musk and she found herself breathing it in like life-giving oxygen. The waves of his hair were all tousled and unruly, the clever eyes inky-dark and gleaming as he came over and stared down at her. 'So when will we see you next?'

Ursula's breath caught in her throat as she tried to stop breathing like a drowning woman. She rarely got this close to him. She swallowed. Sometimes, the lines between their professional and personal lives tended to overlap and become hazy—for her, anyway. Especially on an emotive occasion like Christmas Eve.

She wondered whether he could tell the kind of effect he was having on her right now. Surely he must. He must know that she would fall into his arms like a ripe fig any time he wanted...

'I'll come round tomorrow evening when I get back from Amber's,' she said brightly.

'Good.' He walked over to the fireplace, took a slim, silver parcel from where it had been sitting unnoticed on the mantelpiece, and handed it to her. 'This is for you. Mainly to say thank you for everything you've done for Katy. I want you to know just how much we appreciate it. Happy Christmas, Ursula.' His eyes sparked with dark mischief. 'But don't open it until the morning.'

He had given her presents at Christmas before—but somehow this one felt different. Ursula stared down at the glittery gift she was holding and felt swamped by an overwhelming rush of affection for the man. 'Oh, R-Ross,' she stumbled. 'You shouldn't—'

'And if you tell me that I shouldn't have bought you a Christmas present this year,' he responded grimly, 'when you've somehow managed to bring a huge element of stability into my daughter's life after her mother walked out…then I honestly think I'll grab hold of you by the shoulders and shake you, Miss O'Neil!'

Ursula recognised fighting talk when she heard it. She fought down the tears which were threatening to well up behind her eyes. 'Th-thanks very much,' she said, her voice sounding wobbly. 'It's just that I haven't brought *your* present with me.'

'It'll keep.' He flicked her a questioning look. 'You're getting very emotional tonight, Ursula.'

'It's an emotional time of year. Katy must be missing her mother. Especially tonight.'

He shook his head. 'I guess she must—but any time I bring the subject up, she tells me that she's happy with the situation as it is. She doesn't talk about her much. Not to me, anyway.'

Ursula pressed on. 'Maybe she's afraid to? Afraid of up-setting you, perhaps?'

'I'm not a hypocrite, Ursula,' he said quietly. 'Katy knows that. And I don't play the distraught, deserted hus-band just because people expect me to—that's not my style. I respect my daughter far too much to pretend to have feel-ings I don't have.'

'You mean it's your pride which has been hurt more than your heart?'

He looked at her steadily. 'Oddly enough, I'm a hurt-free zone at the moment. My only concerns are for Katy.'

'And you're worried she's bottling everything up in-side?'

'I honestly don't think she is—she seems genuinely happy. Maybe things are better for her this way. Jane and I always tried to maintain an air of civility between us, but perhaps the underlying tension was always there. And maybe Katy was more sensitive to that than we thought. She's been quite talkative about the forthcoming trip to Prague.' He gave her a slow smile. 'She's delighted that you're coming with us, by the way.' He paused. 'And so am I.'

'It's going to be my trip of a lifetime,' she told him candidly. 'But we ought to be careful, Ross—'

His eyes darkened. 'Just what are you suggesting, Ursula?' he mocked softly.

'Well, certainly not what *you* seem to be implying!' she retorted, then spoilt it all by blushing. 'I just don't want her thinking of me as a…substitute mother, that's all.' She dipped her head to hide her face and a tendril of hair flopped forward. 'It would be so easy for her to do.'

'I know it would.' His voice sounded thoughtful, and unexpectedly he reached his hand out and brushed away the dark lock of hair which lay curled on her cheek. 'Easy for me, too.'

Ursula looked up at him, her expression of disbelief dissolving into one of acute pleasure as he touched her. How could a gesture be so innocent and yet so provocative? Yet surely she was overreacting? His fingertips were barely making contact with her skin, but, *oh*, she could have melted in a pool at his feet.

He let his hand rest there for a moment. 'As you said, it's an emotional time of year. I think it might be better to say goodnight now, rather than run the risk of getting into something we both might regret in the morning.' And he moved his hand away from her face.

She blinked rapidly to conceal her disappointment, but he was right—of *course* he was right.

'I'd better go, then,' she said, dying for him to tell her that, no, he couldn't bear to let her go. To take her in his arms and kiss her until she was breathless with kissing.

'Yes, go, Ursula!' he agreed, and suddenly he looked angry. 'Just *go*! For God's sake! When you turn those deep blue eyes on me that way you make me feel like…'

'Like?'

'I don't think I'd better go into how I feel right now,' he said drily. 'I don't want you getting it into your sweet little head that I'm some kind of depraved monster…'

'Oh, you're not a monster,' she told him shakily. 'That's the last way in the world I would describe you.'

'But the jury's still out on the depraved part?' he teased.

Ursula smiled up at him and gripped onto the silver parcel as though someone might try to prise it from her fingers, afraid of what else she might say if she stayed. 'Happy Christmas, Ross!'

'Happy Christmas, Ursula!' he said softly. 'Grab your coat and go home.'

'Just let me run upstairs and say goodnight to Katy,' she said. 'I promised I would.'

'Yes,' he said, his eyes following her as she crossed the room. 'So you did.'

As soon as she reached home, she got straight onto the phone to her sister.

'Amber?'

Amber yawned. 'Mmm?'

'Ross has bought me a present.'

'What is it?'

'I don't know—he told me not to open it until tomorrow morning.'

'Well, then—phone me back in the morning.'

But Ursula couldn't wait. This parcel did not look like the vouchers from a well-known department store which he usually put in an envelope for her at Christmas! 'Hang on!' she told her sister, and ripped off the silver wrapping paper with the greedy enthusiasm of a child.

'It's a watch!' she breathed, as she pulled the lid from the box where it gleamed softly silver and palest gold. 'My God—it obviously cost the *earth*!'

'He can afford it!' And then her sister burst the bubble completely by remarking, 'Considering everything you do for him, he might have bought you something more *personal*—like a necklace, or a ring or something.'

'A *ring*? Or a *necklace*?' Ursula glared at the telephone, thinking that a beautiful watch was personal enough for *her*. 'Why on earth should he buy me something personal when our relationship is strictly business?'

'Strictly business, you say? Yeah, sure, Ursula! It might be from *his* point of view, but...' Amber's voice trailed off intriguingly, as if no further comment was necessary.

'But what?'

'Well, you wear your heart emblazoned on your sleeve

for all to see—you always have done. And it's obvious to me—and to Finn, incidentally—that you simply adore the man.'

'Of course I do,' replied Ursula, with dignity. 'But as a boss, that's all. And I'm no different from anybody else. Everyone adores Ross.'

'Hmm,' commented Amber, making no attempt to disguise the disbelief in her voice. 'As a boss, he's managed to involve you pretty thoroughly in the rest of his life, hasn't he? Working with him from *his home*? Helping look after his daughter for him? You kept that quiet for long enough!'

'Because I know what a nasty, suspicious mind you've got! His wife has left him, for goodness' sake!'

'Exactly!' crowed Amber triumphantly. 'So therefore it's much more than strictly business! It must be!'

I wish! thought Ursula gloomily, before resolutely pushing the thought away. After all, she was a very practical person, and there was absolutely nothing to be gained from wishing for the impossible.

CHAPTER SEVEN

July

'I CAN'T *believe* that I'm eleven next week!' squealed Katy excitedly.

Ursula smiled as she looked at the sunny-faced child reflected back at her through the dressing-table mirror. 'Another year gone by,' she said softly.

Almost a year since Jane Sheridan had left the family home. That Katy could look so happy was no mean achievement, she thought contentedly. Ross's achievement, mainly, because he had coped admirably, slipping smoothly into the role of single father without ever resorting to dishing out insults about his wife—certainly not in front of Katy, anyway. The times he had mentioned Jane he had sounded nothing more than factual, though Ursula wondered whether there were times at night when he ached for the comfort of another body...

She stroked the brush through Katy's dark hair, pulling it back off her face into a French plait. She wished it weren't so hot. The sultry air had made the child's hair all sticky. 'I can't believe that you're nearly eleven, either! Though sometimes you're so grown up you seem like twice that age!'

'And sometimes I'm so naughty I seem like half it!' chanted Katy resignedly.

'I didn't say that!' protested Ursula, flapping her hand in front of her face in an attempt to circulate what little air there was.

'No. Daddy says it sometimes—but then he tells me off much more than *you* do. Though only when I'm naughty,' she added as a concession.

'Ah! Well, that's what daddies are for. To tell you things you may not want to hear but really need to know. Tough love, they call it.'

'And is that different from *true* love?' asked Katy.

Ursula wrinkled her nose. This was a slightly tricky topic to discuss with someone whose parents had split up. She did her best. 'Well, true love is when two people can't bear to live without one another.'

'You mean, like your sister and Finn?'

'Yes! Exactly like Amber and Finn!'

Through the mirror's reflection, Katy stared at her very hard. 'Sometimes I wish *you* were my mummy!' she blurted out fiercely.

Ursula gave her a sad, sweet smile. 'Sometimes I wish I was, too, honey!' she answered truthfully. 'But I'm not.' She hoped the conviction in her voice didn't sound forced. 'And your mummy loves you very, very much, you know, Katy.'

Katy stuck her bottom lip out. 'She lives in Australia!' she answered moodily. 'And I hardly ever get to see her!'

'But when you do it's in wonderful places, isn't it? Remember New Year? In Prague?'

Katy's eyes shone, her confusion at the complexity of human relationships eclipsed by the memory. 'Oh, yes! I remember the fireworks,' she breathed. 'And you came with us!'

'I was very lucky,' agreed Ursula.

'I *wanted* you to come!' said Katy fiercely.

'I know you did!' Ursula hoped she didn't sound too wistful.

'And so did Daddy!'

'Did he?' asked Ursula casually, her heart missing a beat.

'Uh-huh! And Mummy bought me that big cone of sweets, and my tongue went green and then I was sick *everywhere*! Do you remember?'

Ursula vividly remembered clearing it up. 'I certainly do,' she agreed calmly.

'And you stayed in the same hotel as me and Daddy!' Katy went on.

Ursula's heart thumped with a guilt she had no reason to feel. 'Well, yes. I did. But that was only so that he and I could go sightseeing. It…it seemed to make sense,' she finished lamely.

Katy began plucking at the material of her skirt. 'Mummy and Julian kept asking me if you and Daddy were sleeping in the same room—'

'They *what*?' demanded Ursula, genuinely flabbergasted. 'What on earth would make them think that?'

'Oh, I told them you weren't,' Katy put in hastily. 'Well, you wouldn't, would you—unless you were in love?'

'What was that?' came an amused voice from the doorway of the bedroom, and Ursula and Katy both turned around to see Ross standing there, looking unfamiliarly smart though a little rumpled in a pale grey suit which emphasised the darkness of the hair which waved gently on his collar.

He had spent the morning recording a television show which promised to reveal the secrets of the advertising industry to a cynical world. 'You were saying?' he queried.

Ursula and Katy's eyes met in a moment of perfect understanding.

'Oh, we were just talking about love,' said Katy innocently.

Dark eyes sparked an interested query in Ursula's direction. 'Really?' he murmured.

'The tough love of parenting,' added Ursula immediately, in case he got the wrong idea. Or the right one. 'Actually, we were talking about Katy's birthday before that.'

'Oh?' Ross walked into Katy's bedroom, slowly unknotting his tie. He looked questioningly at his daughter as he shrugged out of his suit jacket. 'Any ideas about what you want to do?'

'I've decided I don't want a party this year, Daddy,' Katy said firmly.

Ross nodded, silently meeting Ursula's eyes as they remembered the fiasco of the last one. 'Then don't have one, kitten. What would you like to do instead?'

'I'd like to go out for dinner in a nice restaurant. Somewhere fancy—just you and me and Ursula.'

Ursula went pink. Maybe Ross would think that she had primed Katy to say that. 'You don't have to include me, you know.'

'I know I don't!' said Katy. 'But I want to. You will come, won't you, Ursula?'

Still pink with embarrassment, Ursula shrugged. 'If that's okay with your daddy.'

'Of course it is,' murmured Ross, and his eyes danced as they rested on the high colour in Ursula's cheeks. 'You look terribly hot, Ursula.'

'Well, maybe that's because I *am* hot!' said Ursula, feeling a bead of sweat begin to trickle a slow path down towards her breasts. 'It's July, for heaven's sake—and we're in the middle of the biggest heatwave this decade. What do you expect?'

'You should try wearing something cooler,' he advised her critically, his dark eyes narrowing as he took in her denim skirt and tee shirt.

'What—something cool, like your suit?' she asked sweetly.

'Yeah, why not? You'd look pretty good in a man's suit!' he quipped, and then narrowed his eyes as he appeared to give this some thought. 'The severe, masculine cut would look rather fetching if it was shaped by those curves.'

Ursula didn't have a clue how to respond to what sounded awfully like a compliment. She heard the shrill ring of the doorbell with something approaching relief.

'That'll be Sophie-Jo!' said Katy. 'And I'm supposed to be ready!'

'You are ready,' said Ursula. 'I've packed a bag, and your swimming stuff.'

Ross raised his eyebrows at them questioningly.

'Sophie-Jo's mother is taking the two of them swimming and then out for afternoon tea,' explained Ursula.

'And I'm staying the night!' chimed in Katy. 'Don't you remember me asking you, Daddy?'

Ross frowned. 'Possibly. I've had my head so full of a new campaign this week it's a wonder I managed to remember to get out of bed this morning! Come on, then, kitten—I'll come and see you out,' said Ross, following Katy as she went clattering out of the bedroom. Just by the door, he halted and shot another glance at Ursula's flushed cheeks. 'Come on down,' he purred, 'and I'll fix you something cool to drink.'

After he'd gone, Ursula risked a look in the mirror. She didn't look hot—she looked frightful! No matter what she did with her hair on a day like this, it was simply too thick and too long to do anything other than lie like a heavy weight piled up on top of her head. Her cleavage felt all clammy, too—but that was one of the drawbacks of having large breasts.

On a day as oppressively hot as today, every article of clothing was superfluous, really. She sighed as she dabbed at her damp forehead with a tissue and then went down-stairs to find Ross.

He was in the kitchen, adding tons of ice to a glass jug of lemon barley water, and already the frosting had begun to trickle enticingly down the side.

He glanced up as she walked in. 'Ready for this?'

'It's making me cool just looking at it!'

He pulled the tie from around his neck and dropped it over the back of a chair, on which was sitting an upmarket carrier bag. He peered inside to see a hat made of palest blue silk.

'And what's this?' He frowned.

Ursula had spent far too much money on it to tolerate any criticism. 'You mean you've never seen a hat before?'

'Never one with quite such an outrageous brim,' he answered gravely. 'You've obviously bought it to wear to Amber's wedding.'

'That's right.'

'It's next weekend, isn't it? And she's going to be wearing the famous wedding dress of your mother's which some enterprising man has tracked down—'

'Yep. That's right.' Ursula drew in a deep breath and mentally crossed her fingers. 'You know they meant it when they invited you along—she and Finn would love you to come. And Katy, too. The Irish are very welcoming to children.'

'Yeah.' He stared into space. 'Sweet of them.'

'Well, why *don't* you come, then, Ross? It'll be a lovely weekend away in Ireland.'

'I'm hardly their best mate, am I?'

'No, but that's not the real reason you don't want to go, is it?' she challenged.

He shook his head slowly. 'No, it's not. I'm not really into wedding mode just now—if you must know. And I'd hate to spoil their day by adopting a negative stance throughout the ceremony. Like when they ask if there's any just cause or impediment—' his eyes glittered with mischief '—you don't want me leaping to my feet yelling, "For God's sake, don't do it—it's a flawed institution!" Do you?'

'Er, no! It wouldn't really make their day.' She hesitated. 'Is that what you think it is, then?'

He considered her question carefully. 'No. Not really. I'm just being a hardened old cynic. I'm told that a good marriage is—'

'Made in heaven?'

He shrugged. 'Maybe.'

He picked up the tray of drinks. 'Come on—let's take these outside onto the veranda.'

Ursula followed him outside to the where the veranda was shaded by the lime-green canopy of an overhanging vine. Ross put the tray on the table and Ursula sat down while he poured them both a drink.

They drank in silence for a moment, the easy kind of silence they had always shared, but the conversation they had just had in the kitchen made Ursula realise that one day his feelings of cynicism and disillusionment would disappear. Then he would be ready—no, *willing*—to begin another long-term relationship. And where would that leave *her*?

So much had happened in the year since Jane Sheridan had walked out and yet—fundamentally—nothing really seemed to have altered except that, if anything, she felt even closer to him than she had done before. He had been right about the ease with which they could switch work from Soho to Hampstead whenever they needed to. But maybe that had a lot to do with the fact that they were both committed to making sure that Katy's life ran smoothly.

Meanwhile, nothing had really been resolved in terms of his marriage.

Jane was still in Australia with Julian Stringer. She hadn't seen her daughter since the trip to Prague immediately after Christmas, and contact was limited to the occasional fax or letter or the odd phone call at funny times, because Jane claimed she could never remember the time difference properly.

Ursula sometimes wondered whether Ross cared more than he ever admitted to.

His eyes narrowed in her direction. 'And what are you looking so fierce about?'

'Nothing.'

'Ursula, sometimes all the shutters on your face come tumbling down—like now. *Something's* bothering you.'

'It's none of my business.'

'Oh, I see.' He threw her a knowing look, iced with mockery. 'You want to know why solicitors' letters haven't been winging their way over the great divide? Why I haven't petitioned Jane for desertion? Or filed for divorce yet?'

'I...well...*yes*,' she told him honestly.

'Well, I *have* taken legal advice, if you must know.'

'You have?'

'Uh-huh.' He leaned back in the garden chair and stared up at the vast blue dome of the cloudless sky. 'And the advice I've been given is to do...nothing.'

'Nothing?' asked Ursula blankly. 'But isn't that a bit like being in limbo? Just waiting...?'

'Waiting's fine. I don't want things turning nasty,' he murmured. 'Or rather, I don't want Jane feeling that I'm backing her into a corner and pressurising her into making a decision about Katy's welfare. Because Katy's doing fine, too.'

Ursula sipped her drink; it was icy and sharp and delicious. 'She's more than fine—she's fantastic!'

He smiled. 'Remember Prague?'

'Of course I remember Prague,' she answered softly.

The three of them had flown there after Christmas to meet up with Jane. Julian's band had been playing a gig in the city on New Year's Eve, and it had been Jane's first time back in Europe since she had left England.

Ursula, Ross and Katy had arrived from London on a snowy December afternoon. To Ursula it had been the trip of a lifetime—but maybe that was because she hadn't travelled enough to get blasé about it. Or maybe it was just because Ross had been there with her. And Katy.

It had been bitterly cold, the skies crisp and clear—with a thick, white mantle of snow clothing the beautiful ancient buildings.

At first Ursula had been uneasy about her presence on such an emotional reunion—scared of being in the way, afraid of doing or saying the wrong thing. But Katy had wanted her there and so had Ross.

Katy, she suspected, had needed a third person present in case her parents began to argue. Ross's reasons had been more practical—he had claimed that he'd simply wanted someone to sightsee with while Katy had been with her mother. There must have been tens of women who would have eagerly offered to accompany him, and Ursula had said so. His reply had been direct and honest, but less than flattering.

'If I ask another woman, then she'll expect more than I'm prepared to give. And I don't want to take anybody to bed right now,' he had explained, completely ignoring Ursula's horrified expression. 'Besides—there isn't any other woman who hits it off with my daughter the way you do.'

'Thanks very much,' Ursula had replied, not sure whether to be flattered or insulted.

But it had been the best time of her life, like every fantasy come true—bar the ultimate one. Because he hadn't taken her in his arms and kissed her. It had been too easy to imagine what life would be like if she were the woman in his life. And that was the trouble with day-dreams—they left you deeply dissatisfied.

He was looking at her now expectantly.

'Going to Prague was an experience I'll never forget,' she told him carefully. 'It was the most gorgeous—'

But he shook his tousled head. 'I don't need a travelogue of the place! I know all that,' he interrupted impatiently. 'But do you remember how Jane was?'

Of course Ursula remembered; how could she not?

Jane had been like a child. A beautiful, spoilt child who had seemed to view her daughter as she would a doll or a pretty plaything. To Ursula it had been inexplicable that Jane should not have wanted to make up for lost time and spend every waking moment with her daughter.

But Jane had not. She had wanted Katy only on her terms and at her times. All dressed up in a party frock to take to the ballet, or decorously drinking hot chocolate with her in Wenceslas Square. Katy as a dinky accessory, with little opportunity to pour out all her hopes and fears.

Afterwards, Ursula had tried to tell herself that she was not in a position to sit in judgement. That she was too involved to be impartial.

'Well?' Ross demanded.

Was there a diplomatic way to say that she thought his wife was a lousy mother? 'I thought that Jane seemed rather—distracted,' said Ursula carefully.

'Yes? And?'

Ursula shifted uncomfortably in her seat. 'What else do you want me to say, Ross?'

'You could try being truthful with me.' His eyes had never looked darker than they did at that moment. 'Hell, Ursula,' he said exasperatedly. 'Whatever happened to honesty? I used to be able to ask you something and you'd always shoot straight from the hip—whether I liked what you were going to say or not!'

Ursula put her glass down on the table. 'That's not fair! You used to ask me whether an advert worked, or whether I thought a slogan was snappy enough, and that's different—'

'*How?*' he demanded.

'You've just asked my opinion on how I thought your wife had behaved—'

'And is that so very difficult to answer?'

She shook her head, knowing that evasion wasn't what he wanted from her. 'Not difficult—just slightly embarrassing. But if you want my honest opinion, then I'll give it to you. I just couldn't understand why she didn't want to spend more time with Katy.'

His mouth hardened. 'She never was a hands-on mother.'

'No.' And then the burning questions came blurting out, before she could stop them, or stop to think about the consequences of asking them. 'Oh, why did you get married in the first place, Ross? Did you love her so much? I mean—I know that Jane was pregnant, but it couldn't have been just that. Yes, you're a decent man—but even you wouldn't surely have married a woman if you didn't feel *something*!'

His laugh was cold, and the hollow sound of it chilled Ursula to the bone, in spite of the blistering heat of the day. Fingers of apprehension stroked gently at her skin. She had never imagined that Ross could sound like that.

'They say that the past is a different country,' he reflected. 'And now it seems so long ago that I can barely remember how I felt at the time. I got to know Jane when we were both students. We all used to meet in a pub on the corner which used to play live music. Everyone knew Jane. She was larger than life, with those distinctive looks, and her outstanding talent for design. Nearly every man in the place was fascinated by her.'

'Including you?'

'Not at first, no. Not especially. I found her a little too predatory for my taste, if you really want to know.' He took a thoughtful sip of his drink. 'And, of course, that indifference made me irresistible in Jane's eyes. For once she wasn't being hunted. The tables were turned.'

'How very exciting for you,' she said woodenly.

He shot her a glance, an assessing look narrowing his eyes. 'It was an exciting time,' he agreed, and unbuttoned the top button of his shirt with a lazy precision which drew Ursula's gaze like a magnet. 'We were drunk with our youth and our talent. Both rising stars in our own little firmaments. I guess it was only a matter of time before we got together.'

Stupid to be jealous of a man who had never shown the slightest sexual interest in her. Even more stupid to be jealous of something which had happened long before she'd ever known him. So why did it hurt so much? Why did she find herself longing to obliterate that past of his—wishing that she could score right through it, like a teacher scoring through a page of poor work?

'And how long before Jane became pregnant?' she heard herself asking, as conversationally as if she had been enquiring about the temperature.

'Almost straight away.' He gazed into the middle distance, to where delphiniums blazed as blue as the sky above. 'In fact, that was one of the first things she said to me—that she and I would make beautiful babies together. I think she saw giving birth as the ultimate creative gesture.'

Ursula gulped as she tried to imagine herself marching up to a man and saying something like that! 'But didn't that scare you off?'

'It should have done. But I was too young and too arrogant to be anything other than flattered,' he admitted wryly. 'My father had died at the beginning of that year. He was such a strong, dependable sort of man that when he went my mother kind of gave up on life. They died within months of one another.'

'Oh, Ross, that's terrible.'

He nodded; shrugged. 'Pretty terrible,' he agreed. 'I guess I was feeling rudderless.' His eyes glittered. 'And Jane soon picked up on that. And even though it was extremely unfashionable to want to settle down at such a young age the fact that I was doing it with such a free spirit as Jane seemed to make it acceptable. Both to me and to the rest of the world.'

Ursula swallowed down the bitter taste of jealousy. 'So Jane became pregnant and you married?'

'Yes.' There was a pause. 'And at first we were happy enough. The trouble was that the idea of having a baby was a totally different proposition to the reality. Katy wasn't an easy baby. What baby is? Especially when you're both so young. And Jane had a career she was passionate about— a career she had no intention of postponing, and you could say why *should* she?'

'It must have been hard for her to cope,' suggested Ursula tentatively, trying to picture the reality of a screaming baby conflicting with youthful dreams of freedom and wanting to set the world on fire.

'I think it would have been a difficult situation for any twenty-one-year-old to cope with,' he reasoned fairly. 'But for someone with an erratic personality and a huge, almost overwhelming talent—well, yes, Jane found it hard.'

'But you managed?'

'Oh, we managed all right. People usually *manage*— that's the way of life. Jane slowly built up her business, designing one-off designs which made the acting and music worlds sit up and take notice, while I started climbing the ladder of advertising.'

'And what about Katy?'

His dark eyes were rueful—soft as pansies and dark as raisins. 'You think I left her to fend for herself?'

'Of course I don't! But a tiny baby doesn't look after herself.'

'Don't I know it! We had nannies to help care for her at first, and that was fine—then when she started school we switched to au pairs, and most of them were fine as well.' He saw the anxious look which clouded her eyes.

'Of course, we had the odd hiccup—some of the au pairs Katy simply couldn't or wouldn't take to—but I've always trusted my daughter's judgement implicitly. And just as I wouldn't work with someone I couldn't communicate with neither would I expect Katy to be around someone she disliked or couldn't respect. In the end, Katy decided that she didn't want any more au pairs, and that's when Jane really started feeling trapped.'

Ursula was silent for a moment, feeling a salty rivulet of sweat as it tracked down between her shoulderblades. She wriggled them uncomfortably.

'And do you?' she wondered aloud. 'Feel trapped now?'

'Trapped?' His smile was almost carefree.

She thought how robust he looked, the strong virile body contrasting with the formality of suit trousers and shirt.

'Believe me when I tell you that I've found this whole experience completely liberating!'

When he looked at her like that—his dark eyes glittering with life and vitality—she wanted to get up and run away, to leave the stultifying atmosphere. What was she doing just sitting here, weaving her little fantasies about him? 'It's too hot,' she complained limply, waving her hand ineffectually in front of her face. Much too hot...

CHAPTER EIGHT

'Mmm. Hottest day I can remember.' Ross made a murmured moan of agreement as he drew the back of his hand across his damp forehead. The humidity had transformed the waves of his hair into dark little kiss-curls—framing his head like a classic sculpture of a Greek god. 'I think I'll go and change out of this suit.' His eyes narrowed against the bright glare of the sun. 'I can't believe you're wearing tights on a day like this, Ursula.'

Having him look at her legs like that was more than a little distracting. 'I'm surprised you can tell from that distance!'

'Well, I can tell that your legs aren't bare, if that's what you mean.'

It wasn't. 'But I might be wearing stockings for all you know!' she challenged.

His smile was slow, almost reluctant. 'Oh, no.' He shook his head. 'They're most definitely *not* stockings. There's a distinctive way a woman has of moving when she's wearing stockings. She's far more aware of her body, and so, consequently, are the men watching her—which I guess is the main reason for wearing them.'

'You're saying that women wear stockings just so that men will watch them?'

'I'm saying that's one of the reasons, yes.' He smiled. 'They're cooler too, of course.' He looked at her legs again. 'Don't your legs get all prickly with heat?'

'Don't *yours* get all prickly in those trousers?' she retorted.

'Well, of course they do.' He smiled. 'Which is why I'm going inside to change into something cooler. Why don't you?'

'Like what? Fly all the way down to my flat for a pair of shorts and then fly back up again?'

He laughed. 'There's no need to be *that* enterprising, Ursula. You keep a swimsuit here for when you take Katy swimming, don't you?' he asked her, his gaze as steady as his voice. 'I know you do.'

It was a curiously intimate observation, and it made her aware of a pulse which had suddenly started beating deep within her belly. 'And what would I want to put on a swimsuit for?' she asked, looking around the garden with an exaggerated show of interest. 'Unless you've suddenly had a pool built without my knowledge!'

He laughed again. 'Oh, come on! Loosen up, Ursula— for goodness' sake! It's a boiling hot summer's day. People are wandering round the streets of London wearing next to nothing and nobody bats an eyelid. Would it offend your Victorian sense of propriety so much? Gone are the days when men flew into a violent frenzy of passion at the sight of a bare ankle, you know!'

'I wasn't suggesting that for a moment,' she answered stiffly.

'Well, then,' he observed. 'You're always dashing off.'

That was purely so that she didn't base her whole life round him. 'I can't spend *all* my time here!' she objected.

'No,' he agreed. 'But the occasional lunch won't hurt. Like today. Why don't you stay? What else were you planning to do?'

She was *not* going to tell him that she had been planning a visit to the library followed by a trip to the supermarket. Neither would she tell him that she had stashed a bag of toffees in the cupboard and was planning to work her way through them while reading the latest best-seller in the cool of her patio garden.

In the past that might have been considered a sad way to spend an evening. These days she had convinced herself that it was liberated to please herself. Her life was busy and fulfilled—she didn't need to go to pubs and clubs which were smoky and crowded. Or go looking for a man just because she didn't have one.

But she still didn't want to tell Ross that.

She shrugged instead. 'Oh, just the usual Saturday kind of things. You know. Washing. Shopping. Catching up on all the little things I haven't had a chance to do all week.'

'But too hot and too much like hard work?' he suggested. 'While I have a fridge stocked up with lots of delicious goodies from the deli, plus a cool bottle of Sancerre that I'm just longing to share…' His voice tailed off on a note of invitation.

Well. There was only so much temptation a woman could resist. Ursula rose from her chair as elegantly as she could, trying not to look *too* eager! 'Enough! Enough! You've convinced me, Ross!' she said drily.

He had also issued a challenge she knew she couldn't ignore. So she would go and put her swimsuit on and no doubt see a look of horror cross his face. At least *that* might force her to accept the reality of the situation, instead of harbouring useless dreams about him.

The swimsuit was stored in Katy's bedroom and was, naturally enough, plain, all-purpose black. Black had properties no other colour had. Black was supposed to magically diminish fat. Black was sophisticated. Black was flattering to all skin types. As everyone said—you couldn't go wrong with black.

Ursula rolled the protesting Lycra up her body and then

stretched it over the fullness of her breasts, before screwing her eyes up at the vision she presented in the mirror.

Her flesh was milky white—a healthy enough sign that she didn't sunbathe, but hardly very flattering. But at least her face wasn't too plump, and the big sapphire eyes framed by a sweep of ebony lashes dominated her face. On an impulse, she lifted her hand and pulled out the clips which restrained her hair.

It fell like a weighted curtain over her shoulders and down her back, gleaming the distinctive blue-black colour of truly raven hair. She shook her head and it swayed and shimmered, thick and glossy as tar—the movement giving her a slightly unkempt, wild look.

An unexpected glimpse of her rear had her scrabbling around in the drawer for a sarong in sunshine colours of stinging orange and fuchsia, which she knotted around her hips. The filmy material didn't completely obscure her wide beam, but at least it camouflaged it. And she felt less self-conscious with the delicate fabric floating around her.

Ursula blinked rapidly at her reflected image. Not bad, she thought in genuine astonishment. Not bad at all!

Out on the veranda, Ross was opening a bottle of wine, and he didn't hear Ursula's bare footfall as she approached, so that she was able to watch him unnoticed for a moment or two.

She had been terrified that he was going to be clad in little more than a tiny thong—the sort of thing which male strippers ended up wearing once everything else had come off! But she realised then that her wildly inaccurate speculation said more about *her* than about him.

Because of course Ross was not wearing a flimsy little anything. He had put on an old singlet bearing the name of his college, and a pair of slightly crumpled shorts which also looked ancient but which were baggy enough to be cool.

His bare legs looked so long—even longer than they ever looked in the office when they were covered up in jeans or trousers. The singlet emphasised the muscle tone in his upper arms and clung to a torso which was lean and spare.

It occurred to Ursula that you could work closely with someone for years and years and have no idea what their body looked like. Well, now she did, and he looked… She gulped. He looked very fit.

He glanced up at her then, an automatic smile of welcome on his lips which froze there in disbelief when he caught sight of her.

He frowned.

Maybe the shock of seeing her in a swimsuit had startled him as much as she had been startled by the sight of *him* in shorts and singlet.

Only more so. Because he looked really taken aback. Almost shocked.

Ross?

Shocked?

'We-ll,' he remarked as he extracted the cork from the bottle and poured them both a glass of wine. 'You look…cooler.'

Ursula quickly took the glass from him with the eagerness of a drunk and swallowed a huge mouthful. 'So do you.'

She noticed that he'd drunk a pretty big mouthful himself, and that the blistering heat of the day was causing the wine to lose some of its chill. 'Maybe we should have a barbecue?' he suggested, with the determined air of a man who had decided he needed activity. 'How does the scent of fish grilling over hot coals with lemon and rosemary grab you?'

Ursula shuddered. If she were at home now, she would be trying hard to resist the chocolate fudge ice cream in the freezer, but oddly enough her appetite seemed to have completely deserted her. Suddenly there were more exciting things to look at than bowls of ice cream...

'A barbecue will make us even hotter, won't it?' she objected, as she plonked herself down in one of two sun loungers he must have dragged there while she had been upstairs. 'I'm too hot to eat anything at the moment, anyway.' And too het up to risk drinking any more alcohol, she thought, as she slid the half-empty glass to lie beneath the shade of the chair.

'Yeah.' He sipped his drink, and perched on the edge of the lounger next to hers.

They sat again without talking, but this time it was no longer the easy, companionable silence she was used to. Ursula was pretending to doze, but between the foresty curtain of her half-closed eyelashes she couldn't help noticing how edgy he was. He seemed restless too, and started walking around the veranda to peer at the contents of the terracotta pots, dead-heading flowers which had more than a little life left in them.

'Hungry?' he asked eventually.

'Not really.'

'Sure?'

'Positive.' She tipped her head up towards the sun. Now he probably thought she was one of those people who only ever ate in secret—the plump woman always refusing food in public, for fear of being considered greedy.

'Me neither,' he said suddenly, and something in his voice made her eyes snap open to see him staring at her with an expression of intense concentration. A look he usually reserved for when something was perplexing him in the office.

'What is it?' she asked.

He shook his head distractedly. 'I wish we had a pool, that's all. It's too damn hot to think straight!'

'Well, drinking wine and lying around in the sun isn't exactly going to reduce our temperatures, is it?' said Ursula sensibly. 'I'll go and make up some more lemon barley water—doctors are always telling us we should drink lots of fluid in hot weather. We just aren't used to it in England.'

'No,' he agreed slowly. 'I guess we aren't.'

Getting up from the lounger with any degree of grace was tricky in a swimsuit and sarong—especially for someone who had a big complex about her bottom. But even Amber—her gorgeous model sister—had once told her that there wasn't a woman in the world who was completely happy with her bottom!

Thankfully, the kitchen was much cooler. Ursula's hands were shaking as she took the ice tray out of the freezer. She was trying to pop the cubes out when they spilt out of their container and scattered everywhere, slithering all over the kitchen floor.

'Oh, sugar!' she said aloud, and she was just about to grab a handful of kitchen roll to mop up when she heard Ross come into the kitchen behind her.

She didn't move; some instinct made her stay right where she was. She heard him come up behind her and then she started with a gratifying shock as he pressed an ice-cube right in between her shoulderblades. Ursula gasped as the delicious trickle of water began to drip icily down her back, and she swayed with pleasure.

'Cooler now?' he murmured, from close by her neck.

Her voice sounded breathless. 'What do you think?'

He didn't reply at first, just left his hand there until the ice had completely melted, and all that remained was the heat of his palm pressed against her back.

Ursula shut her eyes tightly with pleasure, willing him not to stop whatever it was he was about to do next. Because she had a very good idea what that might be...

He turned her round towards him, looping his hands around her waist. 'I am trying,' he murmured, 'to decide whether I have been unbelievably naive, or unbelievably stupid.'

She didn't dare speak, afraid that she would just blow it.

'Ursula?' he said softly. 'Open your eyes and tell me. Do you feel this too? Something so strong that you can't resist? Or want to resist?'

Her eyes flew open in a mute plea, and he nodded.

'Yes,' he said, and then, 'Yes,' again as he bent his face to hers.

It was a moment that she had dreamt of for as long as she had known him. Her guilty secret. A hopeless longing she had never thought would come true. But the reality totally overshadowed her fantasy and Ursula's untapped sexuality exploded into life with Ross's first kiss.

At first it was just the lightest grazing of his mouth against hers. Gentle. Soft. Provocative. The brush of his lips tantalised—so that when that was no longer enough they began a mutual seeking. Their mouths opened to welcome one another, and Ursula had to grip onto his shoulders as she felt his tongue enter her mouth for the first time.

His hands moved from her waist to her back, stretching out and splaying there, and his fingers became entwined in the wild tumble of her hair. Automatically, Ursula found herself moving closer, so that their bare knees collided like lovers. Her breasts flowered into life, hard and heavy, nipples peaked and pleasurably painful, as they thrust towards his skimpy little singlet.

She clung onto his shoulders, afraid that she might fall, while desire flowed through her like lifeblood and she was rocked and devastated by its power. It set her skin tingling, and her pulse-points began a slow, primitive dance as expectation began to unfurl deep within her.

Their eyelids fluttered open at exactly the same moment. Ross's eyes were darker than her dreams, and they seemed to glaze and then refocus. He looked dazed as he shook his head, like a man who had just witnessed something he couldn't quite believe.

And then he laughed, but it wasn't the kind of laugh which had people demanding to know what the joke was.

'Hell's teeth,' he swore softly, still shaking his head.

Ursula stared at him in confusion, barely able to form the one-word question. 'Ross?'

'Now listen,' he said softly. 'It was stupid of me to suggest removing our clothes on an afternoon so sultry that I feel like I'm on the set of a play by Tennessee Williams.' He drew in a deep, shuddering breath. 'But just because we've shared an office compatibly for the last I-don't-know-how-many years, and just because my wife has gone off to the other side of the world and my hormones are telling me that I'm missing a woman, doesn't mean that I'm going to start something with *you*, Ursula O'Neil! Have you got that?'

Ursula's lashes flickered like a home movie. She saw the dazed look of outrage on his face and flinched. She was the novice in all this, but novelty could be a powerful leveller, and it gave her the strength to whisper softly, 'Ross, aren't you getting this a little out of proportion?' She even managed a shrug. 'We just had a kiss, that's all.'

There was a silence. *'Just had a kiss?'* he repeated slowly. He knitted his brows together in a formidable line. 'Really? Well, if that's your idea of ''just a kiss'', then I'd sure want to know what you're like when you're feeling wild.' A deliberate pause. 'Or maybe I should find out for myself.' He sounded almost reckless. 'What do you say to that, Ursula?'

Without warning and without giving her a chance to answer he began to kiss her again, only this time something had changed.

She didn't know what he did that was so different—she was too dazzled by the kiss to analyse it—but he seemed to go out of his way to demonstrate his erotic mastery. She found herself snaking her arms up around his neck and clinging to him like a limpet, making little moans which were midway between pleasure and protest as he continued his sweet, relentless onslaught.

His hand reached down to cup her breast, a thumb lazily grazing the hard nub of her nipple, and she jerked back with intense pleasure as if she'd been stung, gasping his name in euphoric protest.

And it was then that he stopped. Only this time he stopped completely, his hands falling like stones away from her body, his face wiped clean of all reaction. While *she* felt as though he'd taken her emotions and sent them scorching out of the stratosphere.

Shakily, Ursula reached her hands out behind her and gripped onto the work surface, seriously worried that her knees might give way from underneath her, and she saw from the brief tightening of his mouth that her distracted response had not escaped him.

His eyes chipped a question at her. 'You've been kissed before?'

'Oh, for goodness' sake, Ross!' Ursula laughed shakily. 'Of course I've been kissed before! Just because I'm inexperienced doesn't mean I've spent my life in a convent! Or did you imagine that all spinsters—?'

'Please don't use that word!' he bit out.

'What—convent?' she flared sarcastically.

'Spinster!' he growled.

'Why not? It's true! Women who are thought unlikely to marry are still called that—look it up in the dictionary if you don't believe me!'

'Rubbish! It's outdated, and it has insulting associations, that's why.' He regarded her steadily. 'You've been kissed before,' he repeated, only this time he seemed to be seeking an explanation.

'Yes, I have! Of course I have, Ross—I'm twenty-eight years old, for heaven's sake! I've had my share of tongues forced down my throat at parties!' She shuddered at the memory, and wondered how much more to tell him— whether the truth would make his ego insufferably large.

Yet this was a man who had remained steady and calm when his wife had just upped and left—a man who had not let pride stand in the way of his daughter's welfare. Didn't a man like that deserve the truth? 'But never like that,' she observed slowly. 'I've never been kissed like that before.'

'No. I could tell.' His voice was a sultry caress. 'You seemed to give it everything you'd got.'

'Well, so did you!'

He regarded her thoughtfully. 'You know—I still don't seem to have regained my appetite,' he said at last. 'I think maybe I might do some work this afternoon.'

So that was that. A fantasy fulfilled and smashed to smithereens in the space of minutes. Well, Ursula had had years of practice at putting on a cheerful face. She'd nursed her sick mother and managed to walk the tightrope between hope and despair. And in the midst of it all had been Amber's frightened face, asking whether Mother would ever get better.

'Good idea!' she responded brightly. 'I think I'll go and buy some shoes for Amber's wedding.'

CHAPTER NINE

AMBER and Finn's wedding took place in rural Ireland, in the greenest spot that Ursula had ever seen. Amber had booked the Black Bollier for the reception—a fine hotel and restaurant, run by the most eccentric man that most people would encounter in a lifetime.

It was an extra-special wedding—made even more so by Finn's dramatic recovery from an illness which for a brief spell had had him hovering between life and death. His brush with mortality had only reinforced his and Amber's commitment to hang onto the most important things in life, and their relationship was the most precious thing of all.

Amber wore the wedding gown which their mother had bought for them all those years ago. The same gown which Luke Goodwin had traced for *his* bride, whose mother had designed it. A dress which linked so many lives...

Ursula had to gulp back her tears as she stared at her sister in her wedding-day finery, remembering the pigtailed little girl whose tears she had dried, whose cuts she had tended. She looked exquisite, her tall, model-girl figure set off to advantage by the simple cut of the ivory silk-satin dress. She wore her hair piled up on top of her head, and the silk tulle of the veil fell past her shoulders like a drift of snow.

Amber had always looked lovely on her modelling assignments, but today there was something which added an extra dimension to her beauty—she glowed with the inner radiance of every bride.

Ursula had helped her dress for the ceremony—calming

126

her sister down and telling her that yes, indeed, she was the luckiest person in the whole world.

And Amber—who had been blessed with the kind of beauty which could have taken her to the very top of her profession if she hadn't fallen in love on the way—had turned to her sister and said, 'Imagine that I love Finn as much as I do, Ursula. And that he loves *me* just as much!'

'I don't have to imagine it,' Ursula told her sister gently. 'It's there for anyone with eyes in their head to see…!' Her voice trailed off with a sigh; she was still unable to shift the memory of that unexpected and very sexy encounter with Ross.

She had spent the last few days alternating between trying to pretend that it had never happened and telling herself that it was no big deal. Women were kissed all the time—sometimes even *by their boss*! And that was okay. Hardly a crime. It had been a sizzling and sultry day, and their bodies had simply been reacting to the primitive throb of that heat—at least, that was what Ursula kept telling herself.

But at least here in Ireland there was no need for a charade. No need for her to pretend that it hadn't been the single most sensational experience of her life to date. She wondered what it would have been like if he had not stopped. Oh, Lord…how she wondered…

Amber frowned. 'You are *all right*, aren't you, Ursula?'

Which was when Ursula realised that there *was* a need to maintain the pretence. Especially today of all days. Amber would only worry if she thought her sister was falling even deeper for a man who was still married. A man like Ross…

'Oh, me?' She shrugged, and gave Amber her most tender smile. 'I'm fine. You know me.'

Amber was still frowning. 'Yes, I do indeed—and there's

something you aren't telling me, isn't there, Ursula?' She looked in the mirror and tweaked the wide cummerbund which encircled her narrow waist. 'Is it a man?' she asked casually.

Ursula was a hopeless liar; she always had been. 'Not really,' she said evasively.

'Oh. So it is.' Amber's blue eyes glinted and later, when she was nearly ready, she began firing questions at Ursula. Questions about Ross... 'And did you invite him to the wedding?' she wanted to know.

Ursula swallowed. 'Yes, I did, and he said thank you very much, and gave me the most gorgeous present to give you both, but he's not coming.'

'Not even at the last moment?'

Ursula shook her head. 'Not even at the last moment,' she echoed quietly. 'He doesn't really like weddings.'

Amber nodded, and picked her bouquet up.

The church was absolutely packed with relatives from both sides—O'Neils and Fitzgeralds. At the back of the church sat the heavily pregnant Holly Lovelace, with her husband Luke Goodwin, both looking dreamy-eyed and nostalgic as Amber walked up to the altar. Holly had been the first person to get married in the wedding dress, and now Amber was wearing it.

And, in a way, Ursula was glad that she didn't have a man to be serious about, because then she would have been expected to have worn the dress, too—and, quite frankly, it was at least four sizes too small!

The marriage itself was without doubt the most moving service that Ursula had ever been to. Though of course she was slightly biased! Amber had barely been in her teens when their mother had become so ill, leaving Ursula to watch over her younger sister and care for her. Their relationship had always been an echo of the parent-child bond, Ursula realised.

Until today.

Today, Amber was taking a step away from her and into the future, with the man she loved by her side. And, although the love between the two sisters would never be diminished, Ursula was realistic enough to recognise that things would never be quite the same between them now that Amber had found Finn. Which was just how it should be—though no less poignant because of that.

Ursula dabbed her eyes a lot, took loads of photos outside the church, and flew into Heathrow on the Sunday afternoon following the festivities, feeling distinctly flat.

She waited to retrieve her suitcase, which was bulging with corny Irish knick-knacks for Katy, then followed the crowds of people into the arrivals lounge. In her other hand she carried the wide-brimmed hat and a now wilting bridal bouquet which Amber had thrown straight at her!

She was walking along, trying to feel positive about a future whose landscape suddenly seemed very different now that her baby sister was married, when she heard a man's voice behind her calling, 'Ursula!'

It was an uncommon enough name for her to turn around, even if her disbelieving ears hadn't tentatively put a name to such a deep, confident voice.

She whirled around and stared straight into a pair of familiar inky-dark eyes which looked unfamiliarly wary, and the hackles on Ursula's neck rose without her knowing exactly why.

Taking a deep breath, she moved behind the barrier and walked over to him.

'Hello, Ross. What are you doing here?' she asked, her voice sounding surprisingly calm considering that her heart was crashing against her ribcage like a big bass drum.

'I'm flying out to Rio for a lazy month of lying on a beach!' he joked as he met her wide-eyed gaze with a mocking glance and took her suitcase with an air which was almost proprietorial. 'What do you think I'm doing here? I'm here to meet you, of course! I've got the car outside.'

'Where's Katy?'

'She's at Sophie-Jo's.'

'Oh.' Ursula stared at the shiny floor of the terminal as they walked side by side. 'So how did you know which flight I'd be on?'

'I consulted my crystal ball—' But something in her expression made him change his mind. 'You left a note, silly.'

'Oh.'

He had parked in the dimly lit cavern of an underground car park, though his shiny emerald car was easier to spot than most. He stopped abruptly by the passenger door and Ursula followed suit, slightly taken aback when he lifted her chin with his thumb and forefinger. He looked down at her upturned face, and frowned. 'What's the matter?'

'Nothing's the matter.'

'*Something* is,' he contradicted. 'You look pale. You sound flat. What's up?'

Ursula bit her lip. Ross was an intelligent, perceptive man. Couldn't he at least have a *stab* at guessing? Wasn't he aware that weddings were highly emotional occasions—and not just for the couple who were taking the vows? She was conscious that her face was working anxiously as she tried to stop herself from bursting into noisy, self-indulgent sobs. 'Nothing,' she said again.

'Something,' came his soft rebuttal.

She felt so miserable right then that maintaining an air of bravado suddenly didn't seem worth it.

'Just the wedding, I suppose,' she said. 'I wasn't expecting to feel so sad afterwards. Or so empty.'

'Because it marked the end of an era?'

She looked at him directly then, and the understanding she read in his eyes made her want to continue. 'In a way. Amber's no longer my baby sister—she's all grown up now.'

'But she was grown up before,' he pointed out.

'Yes, I know. But there's something about getting married that sets you apart from the world. They're a unit now—her and Finn—and it's legal. He's her world and she's his and...' Her words tailed off uncomfortably.

'And?'

'I'm redundant, I suppose. I've done my job.'

He pulled the door open with a gesture which seemed to Ursula unnecessarily forceful. 'Get in the car.'

She did as he said, realising as she sank back into the leather seat just how tired she was. It had been a packed few days, with far too much singing and dancing and drinking and late nights. She shot Ross a sideways peep as he revved the engine up and reversed out of the space.

'I don't want you feeling sorry for me,' she told him rather defensively.

A faint smile touched the corners of his lips. 'I don't,' he said. 'You're feeling quite sorry enough for yourself.'

'If you weren't driving, I wouldn't let you get away with a remark like that!'

'So are you going to tell me in detail how awful it was? Or are you just going to sulk?'

'I never sulk!'

'Hmm. Go ahead, then—I'm all ears.'

'And anyway, it wasn't awful. It was quite the opposite.' Ursula closed her eyes and let her head relax. 'There were lots of my relations over there—I never knew I had so many! We all stayed in this fantastic old hotel called the Black Bollier which is run by a mad Englishman. And there was a fiddler playing on the Friday night, and then everyone started singing and so did I. Songs I didn't even realise I knew—'

'Songs that your mother taught you as a little girl?' he guessed. 'Buried deep within your subconscious and just waiting for the right trigger to remind you of the words?'

'Yes.' How clever of him to know that. She opened her eyes and turned her head to see the pale amber lights of the tunnel flashing by. 'And the wedding itself was gorgeous—'

'And did you cry?'

'Of course I cried! Everyone cries at weddings! Amber looked beautiful.' She sighed nostalgically. 'Absolutely beautiful—but it was the happiness shining from her face which was the most memorable thing. Everyone said so. And Finn looked exactly the same—sort of *glowing*.'

'Lucky them,' he said, and Ursula couldn't decide whether the sharp edge to his voice was envy or cynicism. 'It sounds like a fairy-tale wedding.'

She wondered what *his* wedding had been like, and jealousy licked at her heart like a dark tongue. 'It was. I've got some photos in my bag—someone had one of those instant cameras.'

'I'd like to see them.'

'Well, you can,' she answered, wondering why she felt so ridiculously shy—he'd only asked to see a few snapshots of a wedding, for goodness' sake!

He pressed a button and a CD started playing an old Lennon and McCartney number. It was a heartbreaking song and, like all the very best songs, it made Ursula feel it had been written especially for her. It was all about the pain of unrequited love, and it stabbed mercilessly at her senses.

Ursula found that she didn't dare even *glance* in Ross's direction. The physical awareness of him was prickling away at her skin like electricity—the whole atmosphere seemed charged with it. And she found herself wondering whether that simple kiss had changed the nature of their relationship for ever. Maybe for her it had done, but Ross seemed just the same as ever.

She had half expected him to drive to his house, and felt slightly cheated when he turned off and negotiated the back streets before driving slowly up her road and coming to a halt outside her flat.

'Th-thanks very much, Ross,' she said nervously. 'I'm really grateful for the lift.' How *docile* she sounded! 'I wasn't expecting anyone to pick me up. I was dreading that long journey home.' Now she sounded manic!

He switched the engine off unhurriedly. 'Aren't you going to invite me inside?'

It was a sentence he had uttered innumerable times in her dreams, but her smooth and well-rehearsed response had somehow deserted her. 'The place is probably a terrible mess!' she said in terror.

He smiled. 'Ursula, *I'm* the untidy one in this partnership—remember? And, anyway—I've never been inside your home, have I?'

'No. Because you've never shown any interest before!' It did not seem a good time to ask him why the sudden change. Or to question what exactly he meant by 'partnership'.

Ursula opened the door to her flat and led him inside. Everything looked exactly as she had left it—the cushions were all plumped up, the plants all green and glossy.

Several magazines and library books lay in a neat pile on the coffee-table. Her mother would have approved!

'Yeah, like it's *really* untidy, Ursula,' he drawled, as he looked around the pristine room. 'You're such a slut!'

A smile began to tug at the corners of her mouth. She'd spent the past few days telling herself that she could survive perfectly well without Ross Sheridan. She had conveniently forgotten his ability to make her laugh. 'Very funny!'

He began to wander round the room, peering at the pictures on the walls, at the titles of the books in the bookcase, and the photographs in their silver frames. He picked up the smallest of these and looked at it closely. It was blurred and of very poor quality—but Ross had an artist's eye for detail.

'Your parents' wedding?' he asked.

'Yep.'

He screwed his eyes up to look at it. 'You look like your mother, don't you? And Amber's more like your father.'

'Yes, she is.' Ursula felt dizzy and disconnected. All of a sudden the room felt tiny and overcrowded, but maybe that was because Ross was so tall. Or because she wasn't used to asking men back here. Or something. She swallowed down her nerves. 'Did you want to see those photographs? Or would you like a drink first?'

'Mmm. Sounds good. Tea, please,' he said immediately, and sank down onto a sofa which Ursula had never considered flimsy until Ross Sheridan had sprawled his long-legged frame all over it!

'Why don't you make yourself at home?' she suggested sweetly.

'Don't worry,' he murmured. 'I intend to!'

Ursula narrowed her eyes at him. He was *definitely* acting strange. Even now, the way he was looking at her— with that mocking kind of question in his eyes and a smile on his lips as though he was expecting *her* to know the answer to it! Was it because of what had happened between them before she had gone to Ireland?

'Right, then. Tea it is,' she said lamely.

And she left him sprawled on her sofa while she went to make it. She clattered around in the kitchen, finding an upmarket packet of biscuits and arranging them neatly on a plate. She had given herself a real test of determination and will-power by saving them for a special occasion, rather than a bored night in front of the television—and now she had been properly rewarded!

When she carried the tea tray back into the sitting room, she found that Ross had opened up the patio doors and strolled out into her tiny courtyard garden. She put the tray down on the small table and went outside to join him.

He was bending over to smell a rose which was scrambling all over one wall in creamy-white profusion. His eyes were closed as he breathed the scent in, and Ursula's heart gave a sudden beat of satisfaction as he straightened up with a look of intense pleasure on his face.

'Stunning garden, Ursula,' he remarked slowly.

'Thanks.' Ursula stroked some silver foliage and smiled up at him. 'You should have seen it in May—that's when it's at its best, with all the lilac out and scented jasmine still starry at twilight.'

'Are all the flowers white?'

'Oh, yes! And most of them are scented.' She made a sweeping movement with her hand. 'When a garden is this small, you need structure. And because it's small, the perfumed plants really come into their own—you can smell them properly.' She closed her eyes to breathe in the scent.

'So it's a garden designed to appeal to the senses,' he observed softly, his eyes fixed with fascination on her face. 'Or at least most of them.'

Ursula opened her eyes to discover that he was staring at her, and hurriedly bent to pluck a lush young weed from where it had set up home between two paving stones. 'Er, yes, I suppose it is.' She crushed the weed ruthlessly between her fingers and found he was still watching her, and her fingers began to tremble.

'So you're pretty passionate about gardening, are you, Ursula?' he asked suddenly.

'Passionate?' she repeated blankly, because 'passionate' was not an adjective she generally associated with herself.

'That's what I said,' he agreed, his eyes sparking wickedly at her.

'It's the first garden I've ever had and I love it.' She lifted her chin rather defiantly to meet his inquisitive stare. 'Though you probably think that's a dead boring interest for someone of my age.'

'Stop being so defensive all the time.'

'I don't mean to be.'

'I know you don't,' he said, in a surprisingly gentle voice. 'It's a bad habit you've picked up along the way.'

The sunlight highlighted the dark, tangled waves of his hair and filtered through the fine material of his shirt, outlining the sleek, hard body beneath. The small, hot garden seemed curiously intimate, and Ursula's mouth was as dry as sandpaper. She didn't know whether it was due to nerves or thirst, but the thought of drinking something became a welcome diversion. 'Shall we go inside and have our tea?'

'Why don't we bring it out here instead?' He pointed to the white wrought-iron table and two chairs which had been last year's birthday present from Finn and Amber. 'It's far too lovely a day to be stuck inside. You stay there, Ursula—and I'll carry the tea through.'

It was nice being waited on. Especially by Ross. Ursula sat down on one of the chairs and stretched her feet as she watched him carry the tray out. The afternoon had taken on a still, dream-like quality which wasn't simply due to the heavy heat of the afternoon sun which shimmered off the blazing tiles of the courtyard. It had much more to do with the fact that this whole scenario was the stuff of her wilder fantasies.

Ross here. In her home.

No Katy. No Jane. No one.

Just her. And him.

Both behaving in a way which could be described as excessively polite.

Ursula watched like a spectator as he poured tea and milk into china cups. He offered sugar and biscuits, but she refused both and could have kissed him when he didn't say, as people always did say, 'Are you on a diet, then?' But then Ross, Ursula realised, had never made a single critical comment about her lushly curved body. Not one. Ever.

She sipped her cooling tea. 'So how has Katy been while I was in Ireland?'

There was a pause. 'She's been…fine,' he said carefully.

'But you had to think about it?'

'Yes.' He put his cup down and made a face. 'I think she's starting to feel unsettled because things between her mother and I are still unresolved. I guess I should have seen it coming.'

'Well, you can't really blame her for feeling that way, Ross.' Ursula narrowed her eyes, hoping that the long lashes would hide her apprehension. 'She's probably wondering whether Jane will ever come back.'

'Back home, you mean?'

'Yes.' It was something she had wondered herself.

He stared at her in disbelief. 'Do you honestly think I'd have her back—just like that—after everything which has happened?'

Ursula put her empty teacup down. 'I don't know.' She shrugged helplessly. 'People sometimes see an affair as a symptom of a bad relationship, not the cause of it. And maybe if Jane *wanted* to come back, and you were prepared to let her, for Katy's sake, say, well—'

'*No!*' His denial cut into her words like a sharp knife, and Ursula was taken aback by the intensity on his face. 'In the end there's only so much you can do for the sake of a child before your actions become self-defeating.'

Ursula swallowed. 'You mean, you've already tried to make a go of it—for Katy's sake?'

There was a stark silence before his answer escaped from him in a reluctant sigh. 'Yes, I've tried. Obviously I've tried. Or do you think I'm the kind of person who would just fall at the first hurdle and give up?'

'No!' Her voice softened. 'Of course I don't.'

'Good.' He stared hard at her for a moment and then rose from his chair, like a man breaking free from the chains of confinement, and suddenly the small courtyard garden seemed much too tiny to contain him. He looked as out of place as a caged animal in a suburban garden.

Ursula's heart thumped unsteadily as he continued to stare at her, his face in shadow, the dark brilliance of his eyes providing the only relief.

'Let me see these photos of Amber's wedding,' he demanded suddenly.

'Th-they're in my handbag. I'll go and get them.' But as she went back into the flat to fetch them he followed her.

Inside, after the brightness of the summer afternoon, the room seemed so unnaturally dark that Ursula almost snapped the light on. They stood blinking warily at one another across the room, like two creatures finding themselves in an unfamiliar habitat.

After a few moments Ursula's eyes accustomed themselves to the dimmer light, and she fished around in her handbag until she found the photos. She handed them to him, and he began to flick through them.

'Pretty part of the world,' he commented.

'Yes, it's beautiful,' she agreed serenely.

'And this is the famous wedding dress,' he said, staring at one photo for longer than the others.

She leaned over his shoulder to look at it. It was a shot of Amber and Ursula, their arms locked around each other's waists, smiling straight into the camera. With her spare hand, Ursula was holding onto her blue silk hat and giggling. It looked as if she was having a good time. No one would have guessed from looking at it that she had spent an uncomfortable half-hour before the wedding convincing her sister that Ross was no more than a good friend and a brilliant employer.

'Do you like it?' she enquired.

'Your hat?'

'The *dress*!' She laughed.

'Very much. It looks...wonderful,' he replied softly. 'Not that I'm an expert on wedding dresses, of course.'

'Did you get married in a church?' Ursula asked without thinking, but as soon as she saw his face she wished she hadn't.

'No,' he answered tersely. 'It wasn't that kind of wedding.'

She realised that she didn't want to hear about his wedding any more than he seemed to want to talk about it. She glanced down at another shot of her sister and her new husband, surrounded by all the wedding guests.

'Look.' She pointed at a red-headed figure at the front of the wedding group. 'That's Holly Lovelace, the daughter of the original designer—she was the first person to wear the dress. She's pregnant now.' She took the photos from him and began to thumb through them. 'This is a better one of her—see?—and that's her husband, Luke. Now Amber has worn the dress, too. And then it's…' Her voice faded.

'Then it's what?' he prompted.

'Well, it's supposed to be my turn.' She gave a slightly awkward laugh. 'I told you before, remember? I'm supposed to wear it next.'

He narrowed his eyes. 'But you don't fancy the idea of marriage—is that it?'

Was he deliberately misunderstanding her? Ursula wondered. Putting her on the spot so that she would be forced to reveal the unflattering facts about herself? 'Well, there are two pretty insurmountable obstacles in the way, Ross,' she told him drily.

'Oh?'

'For a start—I'm much too fat to even get that particular dress over my head!' She shot him a look of challenge, just *daring* him to make a comment about that. But he didn't.

He just calmly said, 'That's the first obstacle. What's the second?'

'Then there's the small matter of not having a prospective husband!'

'No one even remotely in the running?'

Not unless you counted him. And she wasn't stupid enough to do that. She shook her head. 'No one.'

He began to smile then, and something in that smile turned her stomach to the consistency of half-set jelly.

'What's so amusing?' she demanded nervously.

He shook his head. 'Nothing,' he said. 'Nothing at all. I just find I'm ridiculously pleased to hear that there's no one waiting in the wings for you. But maybe it's wrong of me to feel that.'

'Not wrong,' she managed, trying to sound reasonable—

though the words almost choked her. 'Understandable, I suppose. An unmarried female member of staff is always going to have more time to spare, more loyalty to give—'

'That wasn't what I meant at all!' he clicked impatiently.

'Are you sure?' Her eyes were wide and dark and challenging. 'I won't be offended by the truth, you know, Ross.'

This time he scowled. 'Will you stop putting yourself down all the time?' he snarled. 'Hasn't it occurred to you that when I said I was glad there was no one else I was being—?'

'Selfish?'

'*Selfish?*' He looked outraged.

Ursula stared at him, her determination to be reasonable evaporating by the second as she realised that she was fed up to the back teeth with her role as Ross's dependable sidekick. She was sick of being sweet Ursula, reliable Ursula. Ursula who would drop everything to help him at a moments notice. Ursula who would keep smiling in the face of just about anything. She had supported him for too long—with never a hint of telling him what *she* wanted.

'Yes, *selfish*!' she declared. '*You* don't want me, do you, Ross? But you can't *bear* the thought of anyone else wanting me, either!'

His gaze was steady. 'You think I don't want you?'

'Of course you don't want me! Even if you *weren't* married—which you are!—why would you, when you could have your pick of the most eligible women in London?'

He ignored that. 'And when I kissed you before you went to Ireland,' he said, very deliberately. 'Did you think I wanted you then?'

Ursula might have been innocent, but she certainly wasn't stupid. 'That was different—'

'Really?' His eyes narrowed with interest. 'Do elaborate!'

She wasn't arrogant enough to think that it had been because she'd been wearing a swimsuit and he'd been so inflamed with desire by the sight of her body that he hadn't been able to keep his hands off her. Oh, hell, *why* was he standing there like that—looking so unbelievably gorgeous and talking about kissing?

'I don't know,' she admitted, her forehead growing clammy as reaction began to set in. 'It just was. The heat of the moment and that sort of thing, if you'll excuse the pun.'

'And you think that if I kissed you now it wouldn't be the same? Just as passionate? Just as earth-shattering?'

Ursula swallowed. 'I don't know,' she lied.

'Sure you do, Ursula. You just won't—'

But a shrill, piercing bleep cut into his words, and it took a moment for Ursula to recognise the sound of his pager.

'Oh, great! Perfect timing,' he added, his face absolutely deadpan. 'And just as the conversation was starting to get interesting.'

Very interesting. She met his eyes and swallowed down the great lump of fear and excitement which had lodged at the base of her throat. 'Y-you'd better answer it.'

'I should have switched the damned thing off.'

'No, you shouldn't!' she contradicted, even though she could have cheerfully hurled the pager into orbit. 'What if it's Katy?'

His answering glance managed to be both wry and grateful as he reached into the back pocket of his jeans for the pager. 'Yeah, yeah, yeah,' he sighed. 'I know you're right, Ursula—I just don't want you to be right all the time!'

He read the message. 'Ring Sophie-Jo's mother,' he said, frowning as he began to punch out the number on Ursula's phone. 'What's the betting that Katy's forgotten something—and wants me to go charging straight round with it?'

And he probably would, thought Ursula, with a pang of longing she could have easily done without. Katy could twist him right round her little finger, but his softness where his daughter was concerned made him even more irresistible. As if he *needed* any help!

'She's done *what*?' Ross was staring at the phone in disbelief, and his words shattered into her thoughts like a stone through a window.

Ursula stared at Ross, at the sudden tension which had settled on his body, giving his limbs the stiff jerkiness of a puppet. Bad news, she thought, her pulse racing.

'Dear God!' he was exclaiming. 'No. No. No, don't worry. Of course you weren't to know. I'll be right over.' He cut the connection and his face was dark with an unfamiliar fury.

Ursula stared at him. 'What is it?' she demanded. 'What's *happened*?'

'It's Jane,' he said, in an odd, flat voice. 'She's back in the country, and demonstrating her usual love of the dramatic.'

'Jane? *Back*?' Ursula blinked with confusion. 'But when did she get back? And why didn't she warn you?'

He looked distracted—more distracted than she'd ever seen him, barely seeming to hear her questions. 'She's been round to Sophie-Jo's house and she's taken Katy,' he said in a dazed voice.

Ursula froze as she saw the fear on his face, and the same fear gripped her as his statement sank in. 'Taken her where, Ross?'

'That's just it,' he said grimly. 'I don't know! And neither does Sophie-Jo's mother! I'm going round there now!'

'I'll come with you,' she said briskly.

He didn't argue. Scarcely seemed to notice her offer. 'I'd better phone home first. Jane may have taken her there.'

But his voice didn't sound as though he held out much hope, and neither did Ursula, though she couldn't possibly have explained why.

She locked the patio doors, took the tea tray into the kitchen, and when she walked back into the sitting room Ross was just replacing the phone.

She didn't need to see him shake his head to know that Jane hadn't taken Katy home. His strained face told her more than a million words ever could. She noticed that his hands were shaking, his long, artistic fingers trembling like a drunk's.

Ursula frowned. 'Are you going to be okay to drive?'

'Of course I'm okay to drive!' he snapped. 'And even if I wasn't you couldn't help me, could you, Ursula? Since you haven't even passed your bloody driving test!'

It hurt, there was no doubt that it hurt—to have him talk to her like that—but Ursula bit back her angry response and nodded instead. She was usually calm and unflappable, and these were two of her greatest strengths. Strengths which Ross had admired and depended upon...

Now was not the time to let them slip away. And now was certainly not the time to start interrogating him about what he had been about to say that was so interesting. She needed to be very strong for him right now. And for Katy.

He raged all the way to Sophie-Jo's house in Hampstead, and Ursula let him.

'Why did I *do* it?' he stormed.

'Do what?'

'Dump my daughter just so that I could pick you up from the airport!'

If it was merely a case of picking her up, she wondered

why he hadn't just sent a car for her. 'That's a bit of an exaggeration, Ross,' she murmured.

'I don't think so.'

'Of course it is! Letting your daughter stay over with her best friend from school could hardly be classified as "dumping your daughter"!'

'No, I suppose not,' he agreed moodily.

She tried one last time. 'There's probably a perfectly simple explanation—'

'Katy has disappeared and I don't know where she is,' he interrupted icily. 'And nothing changes that one stark fact.'

And after that cold statement they didn't speak another word for the rest of the journey.

Sophie-Jo's mother had obviously been watching out for them, because the car had barely pulled to a halt when she came running down the gravel path to meet them.

She was a slim, nervous-looking woman, who dieted and exercised constantly in order to achieve a dress size not much larger than that of her eleven-year-old daughter. But today was the first time that Ursula had ever seen her look normal—and messy. Her hair was all over the place, and strands of it stuck to her sweat-sheened face. But it didn't stop her gazing up at Ross with an instinctive little-girl look of helplessness.

'I'm so terribly, *terribly* sorry, Ross!' she puffed. 'If I'd had any *idea* that you wouldn't approve, then I would never have let her go!'

He didn't bother with any niceties. 'What happened?'

'Jane turned up here about an hour ago.'

Ross glanced down at his watch. 'And said what?'

'Just that she had been round to your house and hadn't got a reply, so she thought she'd see if Katy was here—and of course she was.'

'What did she say to Katy?' he questioned tiredly.

'She said that she had a surprise for her.'

'And did she say what this surprise was?'

'Well, no. Not in front of me, anyway. Maybe Sophie-Jo will know—I'll call her. Sophie-*Jo*!' she called distractedly over her shoulder.

'And how did Katy seem?' Ross persisted. 'Did she want to go with her mother?'

'Well, she didn't *not* want to go with her—she just seemed a little confused, that was all.'

'Mrs Sanstead—'

'Clara!'

'Clara,' he said, in a steady voice which seemed to take a great deal of effort, 'did it not occur to you that the parent who had dropped the child off should be the parent who actually picked the child *up*?'

Clara shrugged her bony shoulders and blinked her eyes at him rapidly. 'Have you ever tried telling a mother that she can't take her child?'

'No, but maybe you should have done!' he snarled. 'As Katy had been left in your care!'

Clara bristled. 'She *said* that you knew all about the arrangement!'

'And you believed her?'

'Well, I didn't ask her to sit down and take a lie-detector test, if that's what you mean!'

'Pity!'

With a beseeching look, Ursula placed a restraining hand on Ross's arm, relieved when he didn't start shouting at *her*, too. 'Ross is worried,' she told the woman soothingly, 'though there's probably nothing to worry about.'

Clara nodded, looking slightly mollified. 'I know. These custody battles!' She sighed understandingly. 'It was exactly the same with my first husband—he thought he could just come in whenever he wanted and break the access agreement! Fortunately, he's now remarried—she's *much* younger than him—and they've got a new baby and he hasn't really got time for Sophie-Jo any more.'

Ursula saw Ross flinch with distaste, and she was relieved when Sophie-Jo came running out of the house, her face full of uncertainty as she looked to each of the grown-ups for information.

Ursula liked Sophie-Jo. She also thought that *she* was better equipped to deal with her right now than a Ross who was only barely holding onto his temper.

'Darling—do you know where Katy's mummy has taken her?'

Sophie-Jo bit her lip and shook her head. 'She didn't say.' She looked at Ursula curiously. 'Is Katy all right?'

'Katy's *fine!*' soothed Ursula, uttering up a silent prayer that her words were true. 'You know how paranoid we grown-ups can get when you children go off without saying anything!'

'Yeah!' grinned Sophie-Jo sheepishly. 'Can you tell her to call me when she gets back?'

'Sure.' Ursula quashed the possibility that she might *not* come back, and looked into Ross's hard, frozen face. 'We'd better get back to the house, Ross,' she suggested gently. 'At least Jane knows she can contact you there.'

He nodded, and swung away without another word, leaving Ursula to fix Clara Sanstead with an apologetic smile. 'We'll ring you when we hear anything.'

Clara nodded, but her attention was all on Ross's retreating frame. There was a dark spark of unmistakable hunger in the woman's eyes, and Ursula felt quite sick. How on earth could she be eying Ross up and down at a time like this?

Ross put his foot down hard on the accelerator on the journey home.

'You'll get stopped,' Ursula told him calmly.

'Good!'

'It won't do Katy much good if you get a ticket for speeding—'

'No, but it might make *me* feel better!' There was a squeal as he was forced to brake rapidly, and Ursula heard him take in a great lungful of air as he slowed down to something approaching normal limits.

'I'm sorry,' he said eventually.

'If using me as a verbal punch-bag makes you feel better, Mr Sheridan—then please feel free!'

He shot her a look. 'Is that what I'm doing?'

'It doesn't matter.' There. She'd done it again! Reliable Ursula and now…punch-bag Ursula. Great!

'It does matter,' he said stubbornly.

'Okay, it *does*! So don't do it again!'

The house was empty. Ross went straight into the study and came straight out again, and she only needed to look at his face to know what he was going to say next.

'No messages,' he said flatly.

Ursula drew a deep breath. 'Well, let's try and think this through logically. Any idea where Jane might have taken her? Any relatives who she could have visited?'

He shook his head. 'She's got some cousins in the north of Scotland—but she hates them.'

'It's not exactly local, either,' Ursula mused. 'Maybe she *has* just taken Katy out for a surprise. Why not? A trip to the theatre, perhaps—or out to one of the amusement parks. Maybe they've gone shopping?'

He shook his head. 'No. That's just not Jane's style. If she was going to give Katy a treat, she'd make damned sure that the whole world knew about it first. And why the secrecy, if that was the case? Why not just ring me up and tell me? I didn't even know she was back in the country, until...*hell*!' he exploded suddenly, and ran straight back into the study.

This time when he came back out he looked marginally better. 'Katy's passport is still in the drawer.'

'Oh, thank God,' breathed Ursula, fixing him with an inquisitive look. 'You don't really think she'd try and take Katy out of the country without telling you?'

He shook his head. 'I don't *know*—that's the trouble! I'm so worried I can't even think straight! I just keep trying to think what I would do, if I were Jane.'

Ursula stared at him. 'I know what *most* people would do,' she said slowly, not bothering to add that it was an option not open to her. Nor to him, either. 'They'd go to their mother's...'

'But Jane's mother is in Australia,' he said. 'And Katy's passport is still here.'

Ursula nodded. 'Then her mother must know something. Surely Jane would have said something to her before she left the country?'

'Yes,' he said thoughtfully, and glanced at his watch. 'Of course, it's the middle of the night out there—'

Ursula shrugged. 'Well, it's either that or get the police involved—and you don't want to do that, do you?'

He shook his head and flicked through the pages of his phone book. 'Not yet,' he said ominously.

Ursula watched as he began to ring the number, and the dark guilt on his face was like a knife stabbing through her. He blames himself, she realised—for being with me. And therefore he probably blames me, too. Oh, please know something, she prayed, as if Jane's mother could hear her. Please help us get her back.

'Hello?' Ross's voice sounded loud in the silent hallway.

'Marian? I'm sorry to wake you—it's Ross. No, no, nothing's *wrong*…well, that's not strictly true. Jane has just turned up out of the blue and taken Katy without telling anyone where she's taking her, and we're naturally very worried, and—'

His voice terminated abruptly as he began to listen, nodding and saying 'yes' at frequent intervals. Ursula anxiously searched his face for clues, but there was none—he looked neither more nor less worried than before he had made the phone call.

When eventually he replaced the receiver she looked at him, a question in her eyes.

'She says the only thing she knows is that Jane was upset by a fax which Katy sent her a couple of days ago.'

'And what was in the fax?'

He shook his head. 'No idea. Either Jane's mother genuinely didn't know—or she wouldn't say. But there's one thing she *did* tell me…'

Their eyes met in a fusion of mixed and turbulent emotions.

'What?' she questioned softly, wishing that she could simply put her arms around him and comfort him.

'Just that Julian didn't come with her. She left him behind.'

CHAPTER TEN

URSULA stared at Ross in bewilderment. 'Run that one past me again.'

'My ex-wife has left her lover behind on the other side of the world,' came the toneless statement.

Ursula didn't feel that now was the time to remind him that Jane was not his ex-*anything*. She was still his wife. She pushed away the paralysing feelings of jealousy. 'And what's the significance of that?'

'You want a worst-case scenario?'

She wanted the comfort and warmth back which they'd shared this afternoon, when they had seemed poised on the brink of some new understanding. But somehow the idea was lost to her now. It was as though someone had switched a light off in his eyes, leaving them cold and bleak and uncaring. Whether they found Katy or not...

He ploughed on, not seeming to notice her frozen silence. 'Maybe Jane has split up with Julian—'

Pain pierced her calm armoury. 'And if she has, then maybe she wants to come back to you?'

'But I don't want her back, Ursula,' he gritted impatiently. 'I didn't before, and I don't now! I've already told you that!'

The words cost her a huge effort, but she knew that they would shadow her life if she didn't say them at a time when they were crucial. Like now. 'But maybe Katy would prefer it that way—with the two of you together, the way you used to be.'

He shook his head. 'I've never seen Katy happier than she's been just lately.'

'Maybe she *acts* happy to please you.' She saw his look of denial and nodded vigorously. '*Yes!* Children are notoriously conservative, you know, Ross. Like you said—they like the happy-ever-after version. They prefer two parents living together even if those parents are half killing one another. And if you don't believe me—then read some of the literature on divorce and separation!'

'Why are you saying all this to me, Ursula?' he demanded. 'Are you really telling me that *you'd* prefer it if I got back together with Jane?'

'Oh, get real! You know that I…I…'

'Yes?' he queried softly. 'You what?'

She wanted to say that she didn't think she could carry on working for him if he was reconciled with his wife, but she suspected that was going to be the case anyway. Because she couldn't waste the rest of her life yearning for her boss—existing in an emotional shadowland instead of trying to find some *real* happiness for herself.

But she chickened out. 'I…just want to help you find Katy.'

'And just how do you suggest I go about doing that?' he questioned silkily. 'Any bright ideas?'

The tension which surrounded him was almost palpable, cloaking him with the dark, shadowy air of the predator, and now Ursula could see the pulse beating frantically against the fine skin at his temple.

Was he still angry with her? she wondered. Or with himself? Thinking that if he hadn't gone to meet her at the airport then his daughter would be home here safely.

'I think we should just wait.'

'Wait?' he echoed blankly.

'For Katy to come back.'

'And what if she doesn't?' he said, his voice catching.

'But she will! She can't just disappear into thin air in this day and age! And you've got to start believing that, Ross! You've *got* to! Meanwhile, I'm going to make some tea. Hot, sweet tea,' she added firmly. 'While you rack your brains to think of anywhere else Jane might have taken her. She must still have friends in London?'

He shook his head. 'Not the kind of friends who'd want to take a child in.'

But Ursula had got no further than putting the kettle on when the telephone rang, and she ran out into the hall in time to see Ross snatch it up.

'Hello?'

This time Ursula knew that it really *was* Katy, because the slow smile which curved his mouth with pleasure was like the sun coming up.

'Are you okay?' He directed a triumphant thumbs-up at Ursula and the smile became a grin. 'Good. No, of course I'm not angry with you, kitten.' There was a pause. An odd, chilly sort of pause... 'Can you put your mother on, please?'

Ursula turned and swiftly walked back into the kitchen. The last thing she wanted was to overhear a blazing row between Ross and Jane. It might inhibit him from saying what he really felt; though by the sound of his voice...

She felt plagued by insecurities while she made the tea, but outwardly at least she remained calm. And when Ross came back into the kitchen she could see that most of the tension had gone from his body.

She didn't say a word, just looked at him.

'Did you hear that?'

She nodded. 'Some of it.'

'Katy's fine. Jane's dropping her off at Sophie-Jo's in half an hour's time.'

'Why not here?'

'She said she couldn't face coming to the house at the moment.' His mouth hardened. 'That's just fine by me.'

'And did she say where she'd taken Katy? Or why?'

'They've been out shopping, apparently. That's all she said. She wouldn't say why she'd pulled such a stupid, irresponsible stunt and I didn't feel inclined to ask her. Not until I have Katy safely back, anyway. I don't want what's left of the relationship to deteriorate into open warfare.'

Ursula pushed his tea across the table towards him. 'Here. Drink this.'

He shook his head. 'I'd better not. I feel too restless to sit here drinking tea. I might just make my way over there now. I could get caught in traffic.'

Ursula nodded, suddenly feeling redundant. Knowing that she had no place in this father-daughter reunion. But Jane had. 'I'll…I'll go home, I think, Ross.'

'No.' He gave her a swift, hard look which made her heart lurch with excitement and hope. 'Don't go. I want you to stay here until I get back.'

And then he spoilt it all by adding, 'Let's try and reassure Katy that everything is business as usual—and that means you being around. The way you usually are.'

'Yes,' said Ursula quietly, swallowing down her disappointment. 'I suppose it does.' Now she felt like some ancient family retainer, a feeling which only increased when Ross slammed his way out of the house without even remembering to say goodbye.

But of *course* he was distracted. What father wouldn't be? He'd imagined all kinds of terrible fates which could have befallen his daughter. That was what being a parent did to you sometimes—put you on a knife-edge of fear. Ursula had no children of her own, but she had been a substitute parent to Amber for long enough to be able to empathise with Ross.

Her task now was not to mope around wondering where they went from here, but to be a friend to Katy, and make her homecoming as welcoming as possible.

She looked up at the clock. She would make a batch of Katy's favourite scones. It would fill the house with delicious smells and give *her* something to do while she was waiting.

She put on an apron and began to weigh out flour and butter and milk and sugar, sifting and rubbing and cutting and kneading—and she had just put the scones in the oven when she heard the front door slam.

Wiping a stray hair off her face with a floury finger, she glanced up at the clock again. Jane must have dropped Katy off early, and Ross had clearly been risking *another* speeding ticket to have got back here this quickly!

She ran into the hall, untying her apron as she went, her smile of excited welcome dying into an expression of disbelief when she saw that it wasn't Ross who stood in the wide hallway.

It was Jane.

Jane in a pristine white linen dress which was miraculously free of creases, with bare brown legs and cherry-tipped toenails peeping out of white sandals. A mulish, steely-eyed Jane, her almond eyes flickering obsessively over Ursula.

'Been cooking?' she sneered.

Ursula became acutely aware of what she must look like as the plastic apron flapped around her. The clothes she had worn back from Ireland had been chosen for comfort, not fashion—and she certainly hadn't been expecting Ross to meet her off the plane!

Some of her hair was scraped back off her face, but wild

strands of it were dangling untidily down her back and she was certain there must be flour on her cheeks. She was so taken aback by Jane's unexpected appearance that she couldn't think of a single thing to say.

Jane clearly had no such problem. 'I guess you need to cook in order to eat. And you sure must eat a lot to maintain that hefty great frame!'

Ursula forced herself to remain calm and not to snap back the first insult which sprang to mind. She must react like a grown woman. She must. 'Where's Katy?' she asked.

Jane affected surprise. 'Oh, so you miss her, do you? I'm not surprised! I expect you find that your presence here isn't so vital when Katy's not around, do you?' She fixed Ursula with a look of scorn. 'Because I hope you don't imagine for a moment that Ross would have even *glanced* at someone like you if he hadn't had the inconvenience of a young daughter to look after!'

'Where's Katy now?' Ursula repeated calmly.

Jane glanced edgily towards the door. 'With Ross, I expect. I dropped her off at Sophie-Jo's just after I rang here. I've been waiting outside until I saw Ross leave to collect her—'

'Why?'

'Why?' Jane's eyebrows shot up. 'Why, so I could have a word with you in private, of course. Find out more about the woman my daughter is so *longing* to have as a stepmother! To discover how you've managed to persuade her to send a fax all the way to Australia, telling me she thinks her father is *in love with you*!'

'A fax?'

'Yes, a *fax*!'

'I-in love with *me*?'

Jane curled her mouth. 'Apparently.'

Ursula stared at her in confusion. 'I'm afraid I don't know what you're talking about.'

'Oh, come *on*! The innocent little virgin act may have worked on Ross...' Jane's eyes narrowed in suspicion as she watched Ursula's colour rise, and then her thin face seemed to crumple like a sheet of paper. 'Oh, my *God*!' she exclaimed. 'I don't believe it! Don't tell me you actually *were* a virgin?'

'*Am!*' Ursula bit back indignantly.

Jane laughed. 'I suppose I shouldn't be *too* surprised,' she said, but there was no disguising the relief in her voice. 'I don't imagine that you've been exactly inundated with offers!'

Ursula let out a sigh. 'Is there any point in our having this conversation, Jane?'

'There's every point!' Jane angrily jabbed a finger in the air, and now Ursula could see that the cherry-painted nails were bitten down to the quick. 'Are you planning to have an affair with my husband?'

'Having affairs with other people's husbands isn't something which has ever been on my agenda.' Ursula gave her a steady look. 'Obviously.'

The look was returned. 'That doesn't answer my question.'

'It's the only answer you're *going* to get,' said Ursula with dignity. But oddly enough the conversation—far from offending her—was filling her with a new kind of strength. Because it was clear that Jane Sheridan actually saw her as some kind of *rival*!

Jane peered closely at Ursula, her eyes blinking rapidly, as though she couldn't quite believe what she was seeing. 'I wondered when his halo would eventually slip,' she commented in disbelief. 'But I never dreamed that it would be with someone like you!'

She snaked her tongue over cherry lips. 'But for heaven's sake—don't make the mistake of thinking he wants you as a permanent fixture in his life, will you, Ursula? If Ross is making a play for you then it's because it suits him to do so. And one way of keeping his home life sweet and running smoothly is to screw the nanny! Even if she's a hulking great spinster like you!'

Ursula felt her knees threaten to give way. Tiny multicoloured dots began to swarm in front of her eyes. Her throat dried and there was a strange roaring sound in her ears, like a train approaching from a long way off. But she wasn't going to collapse, or faint, or retaliate. No matter how tempted she felt. No, sir. Right then her primary concern was not for herself, nor even for Ross.

It was for Katy.

Because Katy was the child—the innocent child in all this. And Ursula was not going to let the chaotic world of grown-ups hurt her any more.

So what would be best for Katy?

'I don't think it's a good idea if we're both here when they get back,' she said quietly to Jane, her voice sounding miraculously calm and controlled.

Suddenly Jane looked uncomfortable—as if Ursula's unruffled reaction had not been what she'd been expecting. Her eyes sharpened.

'So...' Ursula forced the words out '...in that case, I'd better leave.'

But Jane shook her head violently. 'No, don't! For God's sake—you stay here and *I'll* go. I don't want to see Ross at the moment,' she said.

Ursula could understand exactly why she didn't want to see her *husband*, but... 'Don't you want to see Katy?' she asked her in bewilderment.

Jane stared at her, and her eyes suddenly filled with tears.

'You bitch,' she whispered. 'You scheming, conniving little *bitch*!' And she wrenched the front door open and hurled herself down the path without even bothering to close it behind her.

Ursula forced herself to go through the motions of behaving normally. She washed her hands and face and brushed her hair and tied it back, then took her apron off and hung it on the hook behind the kitchen door. She even managed to time the scones beautifully, so they were cooling on a wire rack on the table when she heard the sound of Katy and Ross arriving home.

Now what did she do?

But it seemed that she didn't have to do anything except stand there as Katy flew across the kitchen and into her arms, with the aim and speed of a fighter-jet.

'Oh, Ursula! You're back! I missed you!'

She had missed Katy too—but she bit back the emotional words whose meaning could be taken the wrong way. Especially at a fragile time like this. 'Hello, Katy, darling!' Ursula hugged the child tightly, and met Ross's eyes over the top of her head. 'Did you have a good time with Mummy?'

'It was okay.' Katy shrugged, turning round to stare at her father. 'But she was acting kind of strange and jumpy. What was Amber's wedding like?'

'The most beautiful thing you could imagine!'

'Did the dress look nice?'

'The dress looked beautiful!'

'Ursula has some photos,' said Ross with a smile. 'I expect she'll show you them later.'

Katy sniffed the air with hungry recognition, then spied the scones on the table. 'Ooh—scones! Are they for us?'

'They are.' Ursula nodded, trying her best to behave as she usually would, though it wasn't easy. Particularly with

Ross fixing that dark, unwavering gaze on her, which was making the blood in her veins pound a slow, steady pulse.

He raised his eyebrows as he took in her hot, flushed face. 'Katy wants to go out for pizza in the village. Will you come with us, Ursula?'

It sounded like heaven, but Ursula forced herself to say no. There were right times, and wrong times. Katy had just been through a fairly traumatic experience and she needed to talk it through with her father. Alone. 'Ross, I can't. I haven't even unpacked after Ireland.'

He held her gaze with a look of innocent query—the kind of look which would have melted an ice cream at fifty paces. 'Sure?'

She steeled herself. 'Quite sure.'

He studied her thoughtfully for a moment, then nodded and glanced over at his daughter. 'Kitten, will you—?'

'Yes, Daddy,' replied Katy, with the air of someone who had rehearsed their lines carefully. 'I'll go upstairs and wash my face and get changed!'

Ross waited until Katy had pattered her way upstairs before he walked over to Ursula and stood there for a moment or two, still studying her.

'Jane was here,' he said suddenly.

Ursula blinked back her surprise. 'Yes, she was. But how did you know?'

He shrugged. 'The scooped-up gravel on the path which looked like someone had been running away? The fact that she'd misled me about what time she was dropping Katy off? But mainly from the look on your face when I walked in,' he answered quietly. 'So what did she say to you, Ursula?'

Ursula choked back the tears which had infuriatingly started to prick at the back of her eyes. 'Nothing.'

'I'm not moving until you've told me,' he said stubbornly.

Oh, *what the hell*? Who was she shielding? And protecting? 'Nothing that wasn't true!' She swallowed. 'I know I'm nothing but an underpaid nanny! And I know I'm only part of your lives because I'm so dependable! A plump, boring old spinster with too much time on her hands who's never had a better offer!'

He nodded sagely at this. 'That's what she said?'

Ursula moved away from him to stand by the window, looking down at the garden without really seeing anything. 'Pretty much.' She turned round then, determined to look him in the eye. 'Anyway, it *is* true, isn't it, Ross?'

There was no denial. No reaction whatsoever. Just that calm, unflickering gaze fixed firmly on her face. 'Don't insult me, Ursula,' he said quietly. 'Not without giving me the chance to answer back, and I can't answer back—not here and not now.'

Which was precisely why she wanted to leave. She opened her mouth to speak, but couldn't think of a single thing to say.

He narrowed his eyes as he took in her tense, hunched shoulders and gave a brief nod. 'Okay, Ursula,' he sighed. 'I can see that you want to go home.'

CHAPTER ELEVEN

URSULA didn't hear from Ross for two whole days.

She told herself that she didn't expect to. That he was far too busy building bridges with his daughter. That he wasn't expecting her back to work until next week—so she wouldn't hear from him.

And she was lying to herself.

She *had* expected him, of course she had. So much that needed to be said had not been said. She had been left with a sense of unfinished business, and an uncertain future. His behaviour both before and since Ireland had baffled and perplexed her—leaving her veering wildly between hope and despair.

Ursula felt that she could cope with anything he threw at her—she'd endured enough knocks in life to have faith in her own strength of character. It was the *not* knowing that was worse than anything—because her imagination took her to places she would rather not go. She found herself wondering what resolution this fresh crisis might have brought about between Ross and Jane—even though the logical side of her nature told her that the marriage was almost certainly over.

But Ursula needed facts, not silence. Like a fish caught floundering around in the shallows, she needed to be set free again—and Ross was the only person who could do that.

So where *was* he?

He was waiting for her on the second night as she was on her way home from her French Appreciation class.

Sitting outside her flat in his car, his shoulders all bunched up as he huddled in the front seat, like a private detective.

Ursula recognised the car from the end of the street, and by the time she reached it her heart was thundering loudly in her ears. She couldn't decide whether to pretend she hadn't noticed him or whether to breeze up to the window and put on an airy, indifferent voice as she said hi!

But in the end she didn't have a chance to do either. He must have seen her through his rear-view mirror, because by the time she drew level he had already climbed out and was leaning against the bonnet of the car, an unfamiliar glitter lurking at the back of the dark eyes. Something in his expression both unsettled and excited her, and Ursula's heart thumped some more.

It had only been two days, but it felt like a century since she had seen him. So for once she allowed herself the luxury of looking at him properly, in a way she didn't trust herself to do too often, in case she found herself drooling.

But today she was determined *not* to drool. She stared at him, carefully keeping her expression neutral.

He had clearly just flung on the first clothes which had come to hand—a pair of black denims which had faded to charcoal-grey and a pale grey tee shirt which had green ink spattered over the front! He hadn't shaved, either—and the faint blue-black shadow which darkened his jaw made him look mean and keen and lean. All man. And very distracting.

Ursula swallowed. And found herself asking the very question she had been determined to avoid. 'So where have you been hiding for the last two days, Ross?'

The dark eyes studied her thoughtfully. 'Mind if I refuse to answer that until we get inside? On the grounds that it isn't really a subject I want to discuss on your doorstep.'

'Do I have a choice?'

Her question produced a wry smile. 'Everyone has a choice, Ursula. You could walk into your flat right now and slam the door in my face, and tell me you never wanted to see me again, and I wouldn't try to stop you.' He paused, very deliberately. 'Not if I thought you really meant it.'

And, of course, Ross knew her too well. Well enough to know that she wouldn't *dream* of slamming a door in anyone's face. Let alone his.

And that dark spark in his eyes was starting to make her feel very rattled… 'Wh-where's Katy?'

'Oliver's agreed to babysit.'

'*Oliver?* Mr Organised? Since when did your partner take to babysitting?'

'Since I told him that I had something I needed to do. Urgently. Where have you been?' He wasn't smiling.

And neither was she! Ursula wasn't into playing games just for the sake of it, but who the hell did he think he was, turning up out of the blue after everything that had happened and asking her questions like *that*?

She reached into her handbag and withdrew her keys. 'Out,' she replied succinctly.

'I know that,' he said darkly. 'I've been trying to ring you all evening.'

Something very close to anger began to bubble away inside her. 'Oh, dear,' she said insincerely, and unlocked the door. 'How tiresome for you.'

'So where have you been?' he repeated, following her inside.

She turned around, surprised by the stubborn note in his voice. 'To my French Appreciation class.'

'Oh.' He met her eyes, and his mouth twitched. 'Is the doorman still after you?'

'No. He's marrying a woman from Algeria and going back to live in Marseilles.'

'Hard luck.'

She turned on him. 'Don't even *attempt* sarcasm with me, Ross Sheridan,' she warned. 'Not tonight. I'm not in the mood.'

'No?' he queried softly. 'Then just what *are* you in the mood for, Ursula?'

There was a pause as their gazes fused. A distinctly knee-trembly sort of pause, but now was not the time to respond to the invitation which had deepened his voice to pure velvet. How dared he? 'The truth!' she challenged.

'Ah, the truth,' he echoed, with a faint smile, as he noted the defiant way she was staring at him. 'That's a pretty vast and complex subject... Where would you like me to begin?'

'How about where you left off the other day?' she suggested. 'When Katy disappeared.' Just as things had been starting to get *interesting*. And that had been his word, not hers.

'Yes,' he said thoughtfully, and walked over to the patio doors, where he stared up at the stars which were just beginning to dot the indigo sky. He stood there perfectly motionless for a moment or two, and when he turned to face her again his face looked entirely different. Calm. Less troubled. As though he had made up his mind about something.

He moved back across the room until he was standing directly in front of her, and Ursula found herself captivated by the dark blaze in his eyes.

'You know, it's little more than a week since I kissed you, Ursula,' he said slowly. 'And I don't remember ever being bewitched by a kiss like that before. I've barely slept a wink since.'

'You don't have to say that just to make me feel better—'

He carried on as if she hadn't spoken. 'I was racked with guilt that it had happened, and regret that it had stopped! And when you flew out to Ireland for your sister's wedding I spent the whole time thinking, Why the hell didn't I go *with* her?'

Ursula blinked with shock and pleasure. 'Did you?' she questioned. 'Honestly?'

'I certainly did. I also spent the next few days torturing myself with images of what *could* happen to you over there.'

'Like what? Getting run over by a tractor?'

'Like you losing your heart to someone else,' he glowered. 'People do stupid things at weddings; they fall in love. I thought, What if Ursula meets some devilishly good-looking Irishman who's looking for a woman with a heart of gold and a silken-soft body? Who recognises a treasure when he sees one and falls head over heels in love with her? And what if Ursula falls in love with him—what then?'

'Well, I didn't, did I?' she said flatly.

He allowed himself a small smile. 'No, I know you didn't. Not this time, anyway. But it set me thinking about whether I was prepared to risk letting something like that happen. And I wasn't. I decided it was time to come to some sort of resolution—for everyone's sake.' He stared at a photo of Amber in her wedding dress. 'Do you remember me telling you that I thought Katy was unsettled?'

Ursula nodded, trying without success to quash the hope which was rising in her heart.

'Well, Katy and I had a long chat while you were away in Ireland. I told her that I was thinking of asking her mummy for a divorce, and I asked her what she thought of the idea.'

Ursula's throat tightened. 'And?'

His smile was edged with sadness. 'She surprised me by asking why it had taken so long.'

'Didn't she mind?'

'Part of her did,' he admitted, with a painful shrug. 'The part which would like all mummies and daddies to live together happily ever after. But she knows that isn't going to happen. She also said that she won't let me get married to anyone else without her approval.' He paused, as if waiting for a response, and when there was none he continued.

'So I telephoned Jane in Australia straight away, and told her that I thought we should tie up all the loose ends and start proceedings to end the marriage. We agreed to a swift, no-blame divorce. She seemed absolutely fine about it. But then Katy must have sent her the fax—'

'The one which said that you were in love with me?' asked Ursula, blushing furiously. 'Jane told me about it.' She met his eyes. 'What else did it say?'

He shrugged, his face reflective. 'It was sent with all the innocent faith of a child. Katy told her mother that she was glad I had found someone to care for. Someone who cared for me. And that you make me happy.' He paused. 'Which you do. Very much. You always have done.'

But his words flustered her. They were too close to her dreams, and Ursula had seen enough of life to know that dreams like this just didn't come true. She tried to concentrate on facts, not wishes, and her mouth puckered with bewilderment. 'I don't know why Katy sent it—'

'Don't you, Ursula?' he queried softly. 'Don't you really?'

'She shouldn't have sent it,' she added stubbornly.

'Maybe she shouldn't,' he agreed, with a candour which made Ursula's heart crash with disappointment. 'But send it she did—and Jane just couldn't cope with the thought of there being someone else in my life. That was why she flew over to England.'

Ursula frowned. 'To put a stop to it?'

'To try.'

Ursula's laugh sounded slightly hysterical. 'Even though there was nothing to put a stop to?'

'Wasn't there?' he questioned steadily.

'Of course there wasn't! We've done nothing to be ashamed of!'

'Maybe not. But I've had some pretty shameful thoughts,' he admitted, his eyes glinting with wry humour. 'Haven't you?'

Well, she wasn't going to answer until she had asked a question of her own. 'Wh-what s-sort of thoughts?'

'Oh, thoughts about all the things I'd like to do to you...' He let the words trail off suggestively, his eyes locking hers in their velvet-dark snare so that she couldn't have looked away even if she'd wanted to.

And she didn't want to.

Something in the atmosphere shifted and changed, and the tension which had been fizzing quietly between them now threatened to spill over. Ursula felt the skin on her arms ice into goose-bumps. Something was about to happen between them, and she knew that she had to grab onto it with both hands. Because it was now or never...

Instinctively, she slanted her eyes at him in a look she had never used before. It was a look of pure provocation. 'What kind of things?' she queried breathlessly.

He smiled, his eyes darkening in response to the unspoken invitation he read in hers. 'Well, this, for a start...' He drew her into his arms with an ease which suggested arrogance, but his gaze was soft as he looked down at her and she could read the tenderness there. And that swung it for Ursula. Because tenderness you couldn't fake. Tenderness was for real.

'That's why I've stayed away these past couple of days,' he told her softly. 'I've been holed up with lawyers, and they've been talking to Jane's lawyers. I've instructed them to start divorce proceedings as of today.' He traced the outline of her lips with a fingertip. 'I wanted to do everything properly, Ursula. And I wanted you to know exactly where you stood.'

'And where's that?' she dared to ask. 'Where do I stand, Ross?'

'With me,' he said simply. 'By my side. That's all.'

By his side. The only place she had ever wanted to be. And he must mean it, because Ross never said anything he didn't mean. She rested her hands against the solid wall of his chest, as if to reassure herself that he really did exist. And he did. He really did. 'Oh, Ross,' she said brokenly. 'Ross.'

'I think I'd better kiss you now,' he murmured. 'Don't you?'

'I th-think so.'

He lowered his head to claim her in a slow kiss which was a stamp of pure possession. The world dissolved, until there was no longer any reality other than Ross. Ross touching her. Ross exploring her—his lips roving over her mouth, her face and her neck as if he couldn't get enough of her. And Ursula kissed him back and nibbled at his earlobes and sucked on his fingertips. Just as he was doing to her.

He kissed her until she was breathless and pliant, running his hands down the sides of her body like a sculptor moulding clay, his fingers lingering with undisguised pleasure on the soft, curving flesh.

'Is that good?' he whispered unsteadily.

'It's better than good...it's bliss.' She sighed, her breath warm against his neck. 'I keep thinking I'm going to wake up.'

He pulled her even closer, their bodies fusing, making it seem so natural for her hips to fit snugly into the hard cradle of his. And he gave a low laugh as he felt her shiver. 'Are you scared?'

'Petrified,' she admitted honestly. 'But it's the most wonderful feeling—I can't describe it.'

'You don't need to, sweetheart—I'm feeling it, too.' He framed her face between his hands and looked down at her. 'Ursula.' He said her name unevenly. 'Sweet, beautiful Ursula. I can't decide which is better—tasting you or touching you.'

Neither could she, but fortunately he seemed more than capable of doing both at the same time. Her eyelids drifted to a close and she tipped her head back as he began to trickle tiny little kisses all the way down her neck, but then Ursula was suddenly consumed with panic.

Because she had waited twenty-eight years for this moment, and she wanted to do it properly. She wasn't going to think of Jane, or compare herself to any of the other women he must have been intimate with before his marriage, but neither could she bear the thought of them fumbling around on the sofa like teenagers. What if he couldn't get her bra off without a humiliating struggle? What if the sofa she had bought very cheaply from a warehouse sale gave way beneath them?

'Ross?'

He lifted his head reluctantly. 'What is it, sweetheart?'

'Not here,' she said simply.

He understood immediately. A smile touched the corners of his lips, and quite unexpectedly he bent to scoop her up into his arms. 'Where's your bedroom?'

Ursula hadn't been picked up since she was about seven years old. Although she might not have *looked* the part, the old-fashioned action made her feel like a delicate little flower. But she wanted him in one piece. 'Ross! For goodness' sake, put me down!'

'No!'

'But you'll damage your back!'

'You underestimate my strength, sweetheart,' he boasted silkily.

He had obviously worked out by a simple process of deduction which was the door leading to her bedroom. 'I find myself wanting to kick the door down, in best barnstorming tradition,' he murmured.

'What's stopping you?'

He smiled. 'Now I know that I have you completely in my power, Ursula—for you to have suggested something as uncharacteristic as that!'

He opened it instead, his eyes widening when he saw the bed, which was embarrassingly covered with a number of furry toy animals. 'A single bed?' he murmured. 'Oh, wow!'

'Are you worried we won't fit?' she squeaked anxiously.

His eyes sparked lazily. 'Oh, we'll fit perfectly, sweetheart—you can rest assured of that.' He tenderly brushed Pooh Bear, Roland Rabbit and friends onto the carpet.

Ursula blushed as he gently lowered her to her feet and tilted her chin with his finger, so that she couldn't escape the understanding which blazed from his dark eyes. 'Still scared?' he asked.

How could she be scared with this man? She shook her head. 'Not any more.'

'And what happened to change your mind?'

'You did,' she answered simply. 'You happened.'

'So did you.' He touched her fingertips with his lips. 'And I want to make this wonderful for you.'

'But you will!' she said in surprise.

His eyes were darkly soft with question. 'Do you realise we've done just about everything together? Worked together, been on holiday together, *almost* lived together, and looked after a child together. In fact, we've done everything a couple can do, Ursula. Except make love. And that is about to change.' He smiled and spoke in a spine-tingling voice. 'Do you want to make love, Ursula?'

'Oh, yes, *please*!' she said instantly.

He laughed and kissed her again, and she wriggled with anticipation as he unbuttoned her dress all the way down, holding her breath as he slipped it over her shoulders and draped it over the back of the chair. Thank God her sister's wedding had galvanised her into buying several new sets of underwear! The beautiful foundation garments had given her a new-found confidence in her shapely figure. Today she was wearing fluid silk camiknickers in the same deep navy as her eyes, with a lacy bra in the same colour.

But even so…she had never stood before a man in just her underwear. She tried to close her eyes with embarrassment, but he wouldn't let her.

'Look at me, Ursula,' he urged thickly. 'Come on. Just *look* at me.'

Mesmerised by his voice, she did as he asked, unbearably excited by the way he was watching her.

'You are a beautiful woman, do you know that? Beautiful and delicious. Just like a rich, ripe, beautiful peach.' His fingertips brushed against the swell of her breasts, where they spilled creamily over the confining navy lace. 'All tinged with apricot,' he sighed as he followed his fingers with the soft caress of his mouth. 'And purest gold.'

He pulled his tee shirt over his head and dropped it on

the floor. His belt followed suit, and he was just stepping out of his jeans when one glance at her startled expression made his dark eyes gleam with comprehension.

'It's okay to be shy, Ursula,' he whispered, drawing her down onto the bed and pulling the duvet over them both. 'Men find that very appealing.'

'D-do they?'

'Mmm. They do.'

'And what else do they find appealing?'

'This.' He dipped his head to suckle her, his tongue slicking against the navy satin of her bra.

'Oh-*oh-h-h*!' she gasped.

He seemed to take for ever to remove her underwear, and by the time he did she felt that there wasn't a single centimetre of her that he hadn't touched. And, although she was a complete novice, he kept saying wonderful things, giving her the courage and the confidence to explore him back.

She drifted her hands over the contours of his body, discovering the firm swell of his buttocks and the long, hard curve of his spine. And she tangled her fingertips in the crisp sprinkling of hair which roughened his chest, nestling her soft body close up against the hard, muscular planes of his.

'Oh, baby,' he moaned, and then stopped her, capturing both her wrists within a grasp which was suddenly urgent.

'No more,' he said suddenly, and Ursula realised that he was trembling as he lowered his head to her breast and moved over her.

He gave her time to grow accustomed to the unfamiliar weight of him as he held her in his arms. She felt safe beneath him, her limbs relaxing to enfold and welcome him. She felt the insistent tug of desire slicking her with its honeyed wetness, and opened to welcome him, her body instinctively learning everything he showed her.

And when it happened, it was all so easy…easy as breathing, with only the briefest stab of discomfort to remind her that this was all completely new to her.

Yet it felt so right…so unbelievably right. As if she had been put on the earth just to have Ross do that to her.

And that…

And…

Ursula closed her eyes as sensation made her helpless in his arms. Everything he did to her he did with an air of discovery, his fingers moving in awe over her skin and all the secret places of her body, as though it were the first time for him, too. And his response made her relax even more, so that when at last her body began to shudder around him in a series of little spasms it took her completely by surprise.

And Ross, too.

Because afterwards—quite a long time afterwards—as he lay cradling her in his arms, idly stroking the black silken hair which had tumbled all over his chest, he remarked, 'That doesn't usually happen for a woman, you know. Not the first time, anyway.'

'Doesn't it?'

'Nope.'

Her body still glowing like a furnace, Ursula wriggled even closer and yawned. 'Ross?'

'Yes,' he said sleepily. 'The answer is yes.'

'But you don't know what I was going to ask you!' she protested.

'Yes, I do. You were going to ask me if you were any good, weren't you?'

Her eyes snapped open. 'Are you a mind-reader, or something?'

'No.' He gave a lazy smile of contentment. 'Just instinctive. I trust my instincts around you, Ursula.' He turned onto his side and let his eyes linger curiously on her flushed face, brushing a damp strand of hair off her forehead. 'Why has it never happened for you before?'

Bathed in the dark glow from his eyes, she felt the very last of her inhibitions crumble away. 'Lots of reasons,' she told him slowly, finding a home for her finger in the dip of his navel. 'When I was growing up, men frightened me. I knew so little about them. I'd grown up in an all-female household—my father died too young to be any kind of role model.' Her voice faltered with the memory. 'And all the other men on the estate where I grew up seemed to think of women as being good for just one thing.' *That* had been the beginning of her plumpness, she realised now. A cushioned body had protected her and meant that the ferret-eyed boys had left her alone.

'Later, I was too busy trying to establish my independence.' She shrugged her bare shoulders and he leaned over to kiss each one in turn. 'So there was never really enough time for men. And because I'd lost my father so young I guess I didn't give my trust very easily. There was someone once…but I was terribly young.' She hadn't thought of Martin Doyle in a long while. 'Then he had the offer of a job in America, and…well, I wasn't able to go with him—'

'Because of your mother?' he guessed.

She nodded. 'Yes, and because of Amber. She was still at school then, and she wouldn't have been able to nurse my mother. I couldn't leave them, but I certainly couldn't take them with me. And it wasn't fair to Martin, either— to saddle him with my family at the start of his life.'

'But you didn't ever—?'

Ursula laughed at the expression on his face. 'You can be very delicate sometimes, can't you, Ross? No, I didn't...*ever*! Amber and I had seen too many girls whose lives had been ruined by not thinking through the consequences of having sex. I was terrified, if you must know—'

'You didn't act like you were terrified today,' he said softly.

'That was different.' It felt as if she had spent a lifetime waiting for what had happened today and she wondered if he knew that. Her voice was tentative. 'Ross?'

'Mmm?'

'What was the...understanding you had with Jane?'

His smile was rueful. 'You want to talk about that *now*?'

'Not really, but otherwise—'

'It gets bigger inside your head?'

She nodded.

He ran a reflective finger along the curving dip of her waist and Ursula wriggled. 'Do you like that?' he whispered.

'No, I absolutely hate it!'

He laughed, then sighed. This was a story it gave him no pleasure to tell. 'When it became clear that the marriage was over, neither of us wanted to give up Katy. Jane felt that, as the man, I should be prepared to leave the family home, but I wasn't willing to do that. I knew that if Jane won custody she would offload most of the childcare onto au pairs.' His mouth thinned. 'And I wasn't prepared to let that happen.'

'So you compromised?'

'Well, we tried. We all three lived in the house, and Jane and I were civil to one another for Katy's sake—but that was about it. We did the best we could under the circumstances—co-parenting, I believe it's called, but it doesn't work, not really. If things are that amicable between a couple, then they wouldn't be leading separate lives.'

He picked up a heavy lock of black hair and twisted it

possessively around his fingers. 'Our ''understanding''—
for what it's worth—was that if somebody else came along
for either of us, then we would deal with it in an adult
fashion. We would discuss what options lay open to us.
Not disappear suddenly, and without warning.'

He still hadn't answered the question she was dreading
having to ask.

But she must. 'And was it…was it…a *proper* marriage?'

'You mean, did we still have sex?' he asked bluntly.

Ursula blushed. 'Well…*yes*.'

'No. We didn't.'

Her voice sounded tiny. 'Can I ask how long?'

There was a pause. 'Almost five years.' He saw the in-
credulous look on her face and smiled. 'You're having trouble believing that, sweetheart?'

'Well, I know you wouldn't lie to me, Ross.'

'Thank you,' he said drily.

'It's just—'

'You think it's impossible for a man to live without sex
for that long?'

'I…well, *yes*!'

'And yet you managed to do so? You had a busy and
fulfilling life and sex didn't enter into the equation, did it?
In fact, you've *never* had sex—in twenty-eight years. Until
now,' he murmured, with a look which had her squirming
with pleasure.

'That's different!'

He shook his head. 'Not really. Men can channel their
energy into other things—just like women. And I had my
daughter and my career to focus on. Believe me when I tell
you, Ursula, that I've never been into loveless couplings as
a method of relieving sexual frustration. And you keep
blushing!' he teased.

'Are you surprised?'

'With you—constantly,' he admitted, and gave her a nar-row-eyed smile which was gut-wrenchingly intimate.

She wanted to bask in the warmth of that smile, but she also wanted to hear the whole story. Sort of. 'Separate lives, then?'

'Pretty much.'

'But not a very satisfactory way to live?'

He shook his head. 'No, not really—but, like I said, it was our compromise. And so many people's lives are built around compromise.'

'But how long could you carry on living like that?'

'Until Katy was old enough to decide for herself which parent she wanted to stay with. That time was rapidly ap-proaching when Jane went and fell in love with Julian. I saw it happening. I think I saw it happening before Jane did.'

'And didn't you *mind*?' asked Ursula curiously.

'Emotionally, no, I didn't mind. I have no respect for people who are territorial simply for the sake of it. Just because I wasn't in love with Jane didn't mean that I wanted her to have a loveless existence. In fact, after the initial shock of her going, I was happy for her. My life actually seemed much smoother.

'Especially with your help.' He flicked her a tender glance. 'But I could also see that Jane running off could spoil all my plans, especially if she decided to fight me for custody of Katy.'

'But without this crisis, and given the choice, are you so certain that Katy would have chosen to live with you? Not Jane?'

He nodded. 'Yes, I am. And that isn't meant to be an arrogant assessment. It's just the way things were. Jane could be brilliant fun, but she was erratic. I was always the more hands-on parent, and my relationship with Katy was closer than the one she had with her mother. But Jane's departure could have ruined all that.'

Ursula stared at him. 'Why?'

She heard the anger which deepened his voice. 'Because, even in these enlightened times, the mother will often win a custody battle simply because she is the *mother*. *That's* why I decided to hang fire, because the longer the situation continued, and the more settled Katy became—well, courts are reluctant to disrupt the status quo. If Katy was happy and thriving with me, then it would be pretty foolish to uproot her to go and live on the other side of the world, wouldn't it? Especially if she had no desire to go.'

Ursula nodded. 'So the longer Jane was away the better?'

'Exactly.'

She thought about everything he had said. And the things he had left out… 'So, in all those years, you've never had a lover?'

'Not until now,' he answered softly.

Ursula's heart raced, but she needed to tell him her darkest fears, because if she hid them away any longer they would only grow and flourish. 'Will you answer me one more question, Ross?'

He smiled. 'Tell me what you want to know, sweetheart. Ask me anything you like, and I'll tell you the truth.'

She believed him. She might be the craziest woman in the world, but she had never doubted his word—his fundamental honesty and integrity. Never. 'If Katy hadn't been part of the equation, then do you still think we would have ended up in bed together?'

He looked surprised. 'If Katy hadn't been part of the equation, I think we would have ended up in bed a lot sooner! Because my marriage would have ended years ago.' He traced the shape of her nose with his finger. 'That's not what I was expecting you to say. I thought you were going to ask me whether I loved you.'

'Oh, no.' She shook her head. 'That's an answer which must never be sought—it must be freely given,' she answered proudly.

'Because I do, you know. Very, very much.'

She stared at him, unwilling to accept the evidence of her own ears in case it all turned out to be some sort of ghastly mistake.

And maybe he knew that, because he said it again. 'I love you, Ursula O'Neil—more than you could ever know. And I'm going to take great pleasure in showing you just how much.'

'But why me?' she asked him. 'What's so special about me?'

He grinned. 'Well, I like spending time with you—that's the main reason. You're my best friend. I can tell you anything. And I fancy you like mad—'

'You *can't* do!'

'Wanna bet?' he murmured, and began to stroke her belly in a slow, circular movement which should have been restful but which had exactly the opposite effect on Ursula. She squirmed with excitement, trying to pay attention to what he was saying.

'Over the years you've crept into my heart and invaded my soul and taken up permanent residence there, Miss O'Neil. And the only difference that having Katy has made to our relationship is that it gave me the opportunity to see what love and understanding you could extend to a mixed-up little girl. You took her into your heart when she most needed you, and because of that Katy has grown to love you, too.' He paused, and Ursula heard the raw emotion which roughened his voice. 'Thank you, sweetheart.'

'It was my pleasure.' She laid a tender hand on his cheek. 'And I love you more than I can say.'

He began to kiss her again then, sweet, rousing kisses which were fuelled by commitment as much as passion. Kisses which marked their union and the bond which existed between them.

'What time is Oliver expecting you home?' she asked him breathlessly.

'Midnight,' he grimaced. 'Or I could take you back with me…?'

Ursula was sorely tempted, but she shook her head. 'It's too soon. Katy may *seem* fine about things, but we ought to give her time to adjust. Let's not tell her until we think she's ready.'

They managed to keep the relationship 'secret' for four weeks, until Katy came home early from her tap-dancing lesson to find them standing in the kitchen, wrapped in each other's arms.

'Oh, *good*!' she said cheerfully. 'Do I get to be a bridesmaid?'

CHAPTER TWELVE

'I THINK I'm going to be sick!'

Ursula turned round and grinned. 'I don't look *that* bad, do I?'

Amber shook her head, then groaned. 'Ouch! Remind me not to move!' She stared at her sister in complete amazement. 'You look absolutely and devastatingly fantastic, if you really want to know, Ursula. What kind of diet did you go on, for heaven's sake?'

Ursula stared at her reflection in the mirror, and the brand-new and pencil-slim image she made, wearing the ivory silk satin dress that Mother had bought all those years ago. A dress she had never thought she'd get into, let alone wear on her wedding day! To go with her brand-new figure she'd had a brand-new hairstyle—a blunt-cut bob which swung fashionably to her jaw and made the most of her thick dark hair. Ross loved it, but then Ross seemed to love everything about her! 'Well, I don't want to sound *smug*—'

'Yes, you do!' chipped in Amber, with sisterly candour.

'But I just kind of lost interest in food. I never really found the time to snack once I started living with Ross.'

'You mean that sex replaced food?' queried Amber bluntly.

Ursula blushed. 'There's no need to put it like that!'

'Well, it's true, isn't it?'

Yes, it was true. Ursula's world had changed immeasurably—Ross had seen to that. It had become brighter, sharper, clearer—more real than real. Mealtimes had lost their allure as the focus of her day. Not that she had become an unsightly skinny-ribs—a woman obsessed with the amount of calories she put in her mouth—or anything like that. No, it was just that the rounded hips had melted away to firm curves, and she definitely had an hourglass shape now!

She fiddled with the cummerbund at her slim waist. 'I wish you had agreed to be my matron of honour,' she grumbled to her sister. 'Were you worried that you'd steal all my thunder, that the attention would all be on my beautiful model sister, rather than on the bride herself?'

'*Ex*-model,' contradicted Amber immediately. 'And no, I wasn't. I mean it when I say that no one could take any attention away from you, Ursula, especially not today. You look beautiful and you *are* beautiful. And not just on the outside—you're glowing within like someone has lit a fire in your belly!' She mopped at her damp brow with a handkerchief.

'And the reason I wouldn't agree to be your matron of honour,' she continued, 'was because I suspected that I was pregnant when you asked me—and some instinct told me that I would feel lousy.' She pulled a face. 'And *do* I feel lousy! Oh-h-h!' She clutched her stomach.

Ursula went over and stroked Amber's hair back off her face, the way she had stroked it so many times when Amber had been little and their mother had been sick. 'Better?' she asked gently.

'Much.'

'Finn must be ecstatic,' murmured Ursula.

'Ecstatic isn't the word for it—I virtually had to *grapple* with him to stop him going out and buying the entire stock of baby clothes from every department store within a five-mile radius!' Her face became consumed with tenderness. 'Though I guess that isn't really surprising. His illness made him radically rethink his life. At one time he never thought he'd live to see a child of his own born. And now he will,' she finished, on a note of contentment.

Ursula grabbed a tissue and dabbed at the corner of one eye. 'Stop it,' she gulped. 'I'm emotional enough, and I'm supposed to be getting married in a minute!'

Amber smiled. 'Where's Katy?'

'She wanted to go and wait at the church with her daddy.'

'Not very traditional,' observed Amber.

But Ursula had witnessed enough of the important things in life—pain and joy and loss—to shrug her shoulders lightly. 'Oh, who cares about tradition?' She laughed.

'And how are things with Jane now?' Amber asked carefully.

Ursula gave her dress one final tweak. Even things with Jane seemed to have worked out to an acceptable compromise. She had written Ross *and* Ursula a long letter when she had returned to Australia, apologising for the distress she had caused them, and for the unkind things she had said to Ursula. She had added:

> I realise that there is no excuse for the way I behaved, but a contributory factor might be that I was newly pregnant with Julian's child, and the doctor told me that the dramatic hormonal changes often make women emotionally unstable.

'Interesting argument,' Ross had commented drily.

Jane had ended the letter with the words:

> This time, I've vowed I'm going to be a better mother. I am very, *very* happy now, and so is Julian—and I hope that both of you are, too.

'That's kind of her.' Ursula had beamed, while Ross had thrown her an adoring look.

'You're the kind one, sweetheart. Too kind.'

It had been agreed that, each year, Katy would fly out to Australia to spend several weeks with her mother during the summer holidays, and that Jane would see Katy in England or in Europe whenever Julian was touring...

'Shall I help you on with your cloak now?' asked Amber. 'We're due at the church in ten minutes. And Finn's pacing the floor downstairs, waiting to give you away.'

Ursula nodded as her sister helped slip the hooded cloak on over her shoulders. It had been made by Holly Lovelace, from the same fine ivory silk as the wedding dress. As Holly had said, 'There's nothing worse than a shivering bride at a winter wedding!' And Holly knew that better than anyone—somehow she managed to combine being a brilliant wife and mother with her career as one of the hottest wedding dress designers in the country!

'Ready?' asked Amber softly.

The two women stared at one another, recognising another watershed in their lives. They had each found their mate—a man each would love until death separated them, and maybe beyond that, too. But no matter what—no matter if geography or commitments kept the two sisters apart—the bond between them would never be broken.

'Ready.' Ursula nodded and held her arms out. 'But I need a hug first.'

'Careful of the dress!' choked Amber as she put her arms round her big sister. 'We don't want to crease it!'

Ursula and Ross had debated whether or not to hold the wedding in Ireland—in the same church where Amber had married Finn—so that vast numbers of the O'Neil clan could attend. But in the end they had let Katy decide, and she had chosen Hampstead, in the little church just around the corner from where they lived, where Ursula and Ross had started taking her most Sundays.

And most of the O'Neils were attending anyway! They had flown over on a cheap block booking from Dublin Airport along with Alan Bollier, the owner of The Black Bollier Hotel, where Amber and Finn had held their wedding reception. As Dermot—one of the O'Neil cousins—had explained to Ursula, 'Sure, and we wouldn't miss the crack of a good wedding—not for the world!'

The church was bursting at the seams. Near the back 'in case the baby starts screaming!' sat Luke and Holly Goodwin, with Lizzie, their baby daughter.

Oliver Blackman, Ross's partner, stood near the front—which was fortunate. It meant that every single female in the congregation didn't have to crane her neck in order to ogle him!

And Katy was waiting for her at the church door, in her ivory silk bridesmaid's dress—a miniature, adapted version of Ursula's dress, made especially by Holly.

'Nervous?' whispered Ursula.

Katy shook her head. 'No. Are you?'

'A bit—but I'm enjoying the feeling!'

Amber slipped into her seat as Ursula put her arm through Finn's and stood at the back of the church. They had asked the organist to play 'Danny Boy' as Ursula walked up the aisle, and there was a great deal of snuffling and digging around in handbags for tissues as the familiar music began.

And then Dermot O'Neil began to sing, and slowly everyone else in the congregation joined in with words so full of hope and sorrow that they hit you straight in the heart.

As the voices began to swell around the church, Ursula was caught up in a daze of emotion as Ross turned round to watch her walk slowly towards him, his eyes as bright with tears as hers were. And when she reached him she turned to hand Katy her muff and her prayer book as the beautifully mournful words of the song died away.

And thank God it was only a short aisle, thought Ursula—for if they'd had time to sing the second verse the whole congregation would have been inconsolable!

The song was especially for her mother, who had bought the dress which had now been worn by three women. She wondered whether Lizzie Goodwin would wear it one day. And Katy. And Amber's baby, too—if it was a girl. And maybe she and Ross would have another daughter...

Clutching tightly onto Ross's hand as the priest cleared his throat, Ursula prepared to make her marriage vows.

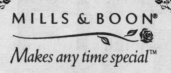

MILLS & BOON®

Makes any time special™

Bestselling themed romances brought back to you by popular demand

Each month By Request brings you three full-length novels in one beautiful volume featuring the best of the best.

So if you missed a favourite Romance the first time around, here is your chance to relive the magic from some of our most popular authors.

Look out for
***Her Baby Secret* in June 1999**
featuring Lynne Graham,
Jacqueline Baird and Day Leclaire

Available at most branches of WH Smith, Tesco,
Asda, Martins, Borders, Easons,
Volume One/James Thin
and most good paperback bookshops

FREE

4 BOOKS
AND A SURPRISE GIFT!

We would like to take this opportunity to thank you for reading this Mills & Boon® book by offering you the chance to take FOUR more specially selected titles from the Presents...™ series absolutely FREE! We're also making this offer to introduce you to the benefits of the Reader Service™—

★ FREE home delivery
★ FREE monthly Newsletter
★ FREE gifts and competitions
★ Exclusive Reader Service discounts
★ Books available before they're in the shops

Accepting these FREE books and gift places you under no obligation to buy; you may cancel at any time, even after receiving your free shipment. Simply complete your details below and return the entire page to the address below. *You don't even need a stamp!*

YES! Please send me 4 free Presents... books and a surprise gift. I understand that unless you hear from me, I will receive 6 superb new titles every month for just £2.40 each, postage and packing free. I am under no obligation to purchase any books and may cancel my subscription at any time. The free books and gift will be mine to keep in any case.

P9EC

Ms/Mrs/Miss/Mr ....Initials ....

BLOCK CAPITALS PLEASE

Surname...

Address...

....

....Postcode ....

Send this whole page to:
THE READER SERVICE, FREEPOST CN81, CROYDON, CR9 3WZ
(Eire readers please send coupon to: P.O. BOX 4546, DUBLIN 24.)